THE MIRACLE ON EBENEZER STREET

CATHERINE DOYLE

PUFFIN

PUFFIN BOOKS

UK | USA | Canada | Ireland | Australia
India | New Zealand | South Africa

Puffin Books is part of the Penguin Random House group of companies
whose addresses can be found at global.penguinrandomhouse.com.

www.penguin.co.uk
www.puffin.co.uk
www.ladybird.co.uk

Penguin
Random House
UK

First published 2020

001

Text copyright © Catherine Doyle, 2020
Illustrations copyright © Pedro Riquelme, 2020

The moral right of the author and illustrator has been asserted

Set in 13.3/18 pt Bembo Book MT Std
Typeset by Jouve (UK), Milton Keynes
Printed and bound in Great Britain by Clays Ltd, Elcograf S.p.A.

A CIP catalogue record for this book is available from the British Library

HARDBACK
ISBN: 978–0–241–43427–7

TRADE PAPERBACK
ISBN: 978–0–241–48643–6

All correspondence to:
Puffin Books
Penguin Random House
One Embassy Gardens, 8 Viaduct Gardens,
London, SW11 7BW

For Louise
The Marley to my Marley

Contents

1. Marley's Last-Minute Miracle   1

2. The Scrooge in the Kitchen   19

3. The Midnight Picnic   27

4. The Insistent Snow Globe   33

5. A Most Unexpected Visitor   38

6. The Creeping Countryside   45

7. The Marley in the Mirror   52

8. The Impossible Puddle   63

9. The Accidental Avalanche   71

10. A Matter of Deliberate Disbelief   75

11. The Out-of-Place Man   83

12. The Hopeless Child   94

13. The Elf on the Shelf   102

14. The Obstruction in the Hallway 114

15. A Highly Unusual Letter 122

16. Code Red 132

17. Not-So-Tiny Tim 141

18. The Accidental Shrinking 148

19. The Case of the Secure Stocking™ 156

20. The Grey Man 166

21. A Gloomy Fate 176

22. The Shattered Snow Globe 181

23. The Devouring Fog 185

24. The Sound of Home 189

25. The Curious Bedroom Shop 194

26. The Most Important Decision in the World 205

27. The Return of Christmas 213

 Epilogue 217

THE
MIRACLE
ON
EBENEZER
STREET

Marley's Last-Minute Miracle

George Bishop was hardly a master of disguise, but he knew how to wear a fake moustache. He traced his finger along his upper lip, smoothing it with the confidence of a Bond villain. 'The trick is not to sneeze.'

The moustache was made of tinsel, and in the falling evening its reflection glittered in Nana Flo's eyes. She tapped the side of her nose. 'When it comes to sneaking, George, glamour is absolutely key.'

The Christmas Fair at Hyde Park unfurled before them like a magnificent metropolis, its fairy lights winking at George through the bustling crowds.

'Call me Mistletoe Marple,' said Nana Flo, excitement quickening her steps. 'Didn't I tell you we'd find it?'

George grinned. 'Well, it's not exactly hid–'

A loud grunt startled him from his sentence. The smile died on his lips as a broad-shouldered businessman jostled past them, the end of his black coat flapping in the breeze.

George stiffened. 'Is that –'

Nana Flo threaded an arm through the crook of his elbow. 'He'd never find us here, love. Not today of all days. And *especially* not in your fine disguise.'

George slumped with relief. Nana Flo was right. It was late afternoon on 23 December, and his father was at work. Just like he was every other day of the year, rain or shine, weekends and weekdays, holidays and all the billable minutes in between. Hugo Bishop wouldn't *dream* of setting foot outside his office, especially not with Christmas floating about so infectiously.

Overhead, the milk-bottle clouds were thick with the promise of snow, the air dusted with the scent of cinnamon. George inhaled a generous lungful as he followed it through the fair gates.

He was happy here in the belly of Christmas. Full of mince pies and candyfloss and the kind of self-assuredness that only a tinsel moustache can bring. 'I think I'll keep it on,' he told his nan on the Ferris wheel. 'It makes me feel important.'

'You do look a bit like Clark Gable,' said Nana Flo, around a mouthful of fudge. 'One of my all-time favourite film stars.' A pause, then: 'Or a festive broom handle, at the very least.'

She adjusted her own carefully selected Christmas accessory: a holly hairclip, adorned with bright red berries and jade leaves. It sat just above her left ear, and made the green of her eyes seem brighter, somehow. Almost . . . mischievous.

Hours later, when the moon was climbing into an indigo sky, and their legs had grown heavy from wonderland wandering, Nana Flo pressed a £5 note into his hand. 'Why don't you run and get yourself a hot chocolate from Gino's.' She gestured to a row of identical wooden cabins that looked out on to the carousel. 'Save me a marshmallow. I'm going to see about a mulled wine, or three.'

George was already off and running. He thought Gino's Cioccolata was the last shop on the little row, but when he reached it, he spied another cabin tucked away at the very end. It was absent of decoration, except for the crooked sign hanging above the door.

It read:

MARLEY'S CHRISTMAS CURIOSITIES

And underneath, in fine print:

Strictly No Grown-ups Allowed
Enter At Your Own Whimsy

The bell above the door tinkled as he pushed it open.

George was surprised to find himself in a room much larger than he was expecting. It was cosy too. The floor was blanketed with fresh pine needles that made the shop smell of evergreen trees. Overhead, garlands of fairy lights hung from the low ceiling, setting a dim glow about the place. A girl and a boy were examining the shelf nearest the door. They were a little younger than George, and were arguing over a bright yellow parcel of sweets.

'Mum's allergic to toffee, you *dunder*brain.'

'You're thinking of *nougat*. There's a *massive* difference.'

At the back of the shop, behind a wooden desk heaped with books, an old man sat reading a newspaper. His spectacles were perched on the very end of his nose.

He peered at George over the top of them.

George lifted a gloved hand in greeting. 'Er, hi.'

The old man – Marley, George supposed – looked at him closely now, his bushy brows hunching together. 'Age?'

'Uh.' George shuffled closer, arcing around a cluster of children, who were chattering excitedly by a table in the middle of the shop.

'Ten,' he told Marley.

'And?' prompted the old man.

'Ten . . . and four months?'

Marley tapped his upper lip. 'That's an unusual amount of facial hair for a ten-years-and-four-months-old. I'm not saying I haven't seen it before . . .' He narrowed his eyes suspiciously. 'But it's rare as a purple reindeer.'

'There's no such thing as a purple reindeer,' said George.

Marley stared at him. 'Excuse me?'

George shifted uncomfortably. 'The moustache is fake. It's just tinsel.'

'I see,' Marley said, unconvinced.

George was distracted by the date on his newspaper. '1843?' he said, squinting to be sure. 'Why are you reading something from 1843?'

'I prefer the classics,' said Marley in a tone that conveyed the word *obviously*.

'Hmm.' The silence stretched, George frozen in place by the sudden, searing brightness of Marley's gaze until, with a sprawling yawn, the old man returned his attention to the events of 1843. 'You certainly are ten and four months old,' he said, with a dismissive flick of his wrist. 'Crackers are free. *One* per child. Everything else comes at a price.'

'Right. Thanks.' George drifted towards the table in the middle of the shop, poking his head between two sets of shoulders to find a teetering heap of Christmas crackers.

A red-haired girl had just pulled one apart to find a perfectly tuned music box inside. Her sister's cracker, meanwhile, contained a live butterfly, its wings glittering silver and gold as it flitted between them.

Beside them, a pair of wide-eyed brothers were trying out matching miniature telescopes.

'I can see a *whale* in mine!' fizzed the older one as he squinted into the eyepiece. 'What have you got?'

'Marbles,' said the younger glumly. He stiffened, then, his voice jumping an entire octave: 'No, wait. *Planets*. I've got the universe in mine!'

George steeled himself. With his heart cartwheeling in his chest, he plucked a bright red cracker from the pile and ripped it open.

Pop!

All four children turned to stare at him as he flipped the cracker upside down, and shook it.

And shook.

And shook.

6

And *shook*.

'You can stop now,' said the red-haired girl, eyes round with sympathy. 'It's a Scrooge.'

George frowned at his hollow cracker. 'What's a *Scrooge*?'

The girl gestured at the foil, already tarnishing in his hands. 'It's an empty cracker. It happens sometimes,' she said, her attention already shifting back to her music box. 'Bad luck.'

George laid the cracker down, his gaze drawn to the miniature sign on the table.

*Strictly **one** cracker per child.*
WARNING: Scrooge hazard.
*Satisfaction **not** guaranteed.*

'That's not very fair,' he mumbled, but the others weren't listening any more. They had returned to marvelling at their gifts, leaving George to his own stirring curiosity.

He wandered away. A row of sapphire-eyed rocking horses peered up at him as he paused to inspect a shelf called JINGLES, which housed an extensive collection of bells. Below it, a shelf called TRICKSIES was packed with wooden elves in bright green hats, sitting shoulder to shoulder. Their little legs dangled over the edge, their wide faces wearing blank-eyed stares and toothless smiles that stretched too wide.

'Creepy,' muttered George as he hunkered down.

He swore he heard an answering grunt, but when he looked around there was no one there. Most of the children had left with their new toys, leaving just the arguing siblings from before. They were stationed all the way across the shop. He decided it must have been the floorboards, squeaky beneath the pine needles.

WHY NOT? included the most impressive collection of Christmas hats George had ever seen – woolly creations with humongous bobbles, Santa hats that came complete with cloudy beards, and stripy ones that wound round and round and round, all the way towards the ceiling. There were flashing red noses and candy-cane earrings, elf-shoes with golden bells on top and an array of woolly Christmas jumpers of all sizes, including one tiny enough to fit a bumblebee.

'But why . . .'

'I think you'll find the question is *why not?*' Marley piped up from behind his newspaper. 'Bees are famously festive. Many animals are, in fact.'

George fleetingly thought about putting Coco the cat in a Christmas jumper, but he could already picture the disgruntlement that would earn him. He moved on, past jars of *Jolly-Making Jam* (one spoon at a time), pots of *Talkative Teabags* (after school only) and stacks of *Belligerent Bath-bombs* (luxuriously insensitive), which were arranged artfully around a big blue tin of *Melancholic Mints* (have yourself a nice cathartic weep).

ABSOLUTELY IMPOSSIBLE housed miniature chimneys no bigger than George's fist, each one made of real brick and sprinkled with soot. In one of the chimneys, George swore he could see a tiny black boot dangling inside the grate but when he poked his finger in, it disappeared. Beside it, IMPOSSIBLY ABSOLUTE was full of delectable treats: gingerbread Santa Clauses, cinnamon-biscuit trees and snowball-shaped cream cakes. Their glittering labels promised *Christmas in every nibble, delight in every bite.*

George bumped into the sniping siblings at a shelf called CHRISTMAS CAROLS. They were poring over a line-up of glass birds, trying to decide between the bluebird and the nightingale. Every time they picked one up to inspect it, the bird chirped a perfectly tuned Christmas melody. On the shelf below, labelled CHRISTMAS QUARRELS, the same set of birds surrendered angry squawks and shrill screeches when touched. After lifting the first one, George returned it promptly and backed away from the shelf, spouting, 'Sorry, sorry, sorry, sorry,' until the siblings stopped glaring at him.

He found himself then at LAST-MINUTE MIRACLES.

It was a shelf of snow globes. There were churches and houses and cities and villages, whole worlds populated by tiny figures twirling in feather-soft snow. He studied each one in turn, his breath catching when he came to the final snow globe.

With trembling fingers, George lifted it from its perch and brought it to his nose. It was almost empty, save for one familiar figure.

'That's impossible,' he whispered.

This time, Marley said nothing.

George peered into the glass. A lopsided snowman stared back at him, with one blue-button eye, one yellow as the sun. His smile was a crescent of turquoise beads – George's mother's necklace. His nose was a bright orange carrot, and on his bulbous head sat a familiar dark green trilby hat, scuffed along the rim. It belonged to George's father. *That was the beginning of my fashionable phase, Georgie*, echoed his voice in George's head. *Sometimes, a spark of colour makes all the difference in the world.*

George's breath fogged against the snow globe.

This wasn't just *any* snowman.

It was *George's* snowman.

The three of them had made it together at Nan's old house on Christmas Eve morning, heaving and stacking and packing and chiselling, their laughter chattering happily through their teeth, while his father's nose turned red and his mother's fingers went numb.

He looks like a Fred, doesn't he, darling?

Our perfectly imperfect Fred.

Somewhere behind George, a bell jingled.

Old Marley ruffled his newspaper. 'Age?'

'Um. Eleven?'

'And?'

A tremulous response. 'Eleven . . . and three quarters?'

George might have recognized the voice if he hadn't been hopelessly lost in the folds of his own past at that moment.

'And the smaller one?'

'Clementine is six.'

A younger voice then, loud as a foghorn. 'SIX AND ONE DAY ACTUALLY.'

Clementine.

George didn't hear the name.

'I'M A CAPRICORN. JUST LIKE JESUS.'

An appraising *hmm* from Marley. 'And are you quite sure you're not secretly thirty-seven, Clementine? There's a boy over there with a fully-grown moustache. It's impossible to tell these days.'

A delighted giggle. 'NOPE.'

There was nothing then but the rustle of curiosity, two satisfying *pops!* and the murmurings of two children utterly engrossed in the contents of their Christmas crackers.

Across the shop, George was afraid to move. He might lose it then – the sound of his mother's laughter, undusting itself in the farthest corner of his mind.

There was a tap on his shoulder. 'George?'

George was so startled he nearly smashed the snow globe. He whirled round.

His cousin blinked back at him. She was taller than when George had last seen her, but her hair was just as curly and her eyes were the same chestnut brown. George would have known them anywhere.

'B-Bobbie,' he spluttered. 'W-what are you doing here?'

'I can't believe it's really you, George.' Bobbie shook her head in disbelief. 'And *here* of all places. We haven't seen you in . . .' she trailed off, a blush rising in her cheeks. 'Well, since the funeral.'

George wanted the ground to swallow him up, gulp him down and then digest him for good measure. 'Yeah . . . It's been ages.'

'HALLO, GEORGE!' Clementine appeared beside her sister, waving a clump of red foil in greeting. 'I'M SIX NOW. DID YOU KNOW?'

George stared down at his littlest cousin. What she was missing in front teeth, she made up for in enthusiasm. She was wearing a scarf made of pine cones and smiling with her whole face. 'Happy birthday for yesterday, Clem.'

'YOU HAVE A CATERPILLAR ON YOUR FACE, GEORGE.'

Embarrassment roared in George's ears as he suddenly remembered the moustache. He whipped it off in one painful swipe.

Clementine screamed.

A chair screeched as old Marley leapt to his feet. 'What the Dickens is going on over there?'

'It's all right, Clem,' hushed Bobbie. 'It's only pretend.'

George gestured at the crumpled foil in Clementine's fist. 'Did you pull your cracker?' he asked, flipping the subject like a coin in his palm. 'What did you get?'

Clementine caught a shuddering breath, and nodded. She peeled the foil away to reveal a tiny white snowflake. 'Bobbie says it's called a *Forever Flake*.' She frowned as she turned it over. 'I don't think you can eat it.' She nibbled at its edges just to be sure, then made a face. 'It tastes like a tree.'

'I got a *Grow-Your-Own Christmas Cake*.' Bobbie held up an iced Christmas cake the exact size of a £1 coin. 'Apparently you just add water.'

George eyed the tiny cake with great suspicion.

'Hey, remember the Christmas when you ate four slices of cake in a row and had to lie down for an hour?' said Bobbie. 'You completely missed Pictionary.'

George blushed. 'Yeah, I remember.'

'Do you still draw?' she asked. 'You and your mum made such a good team. The rest of us never got a look-in.'

'Not really,' said George, struggling to remember the last time he had even tried. 'It's hard to think of stuff these days.'

'DRAGONS!' Clementine burst out.

George smiled. 'That's a good idea, Clem.'

Clementine beamed with pride. 'Why did you disappear, Georgie? We miss you.'

George's throat throbbed with the words he wanted to say. *I miss you, too. All of you, including Doodle, and sometimes at night if I think about it too much I want to cry.* 'Oh, er. Well . . .'

'What have you got then?' said Bobbie awkwardly. She pointed to the snow globe in his hand. 'How did that even *fit* in a cracker?'

'Oh, this? No. No, this isn't mine. I didn't get anything in my cracker. I got a Scrooge. Bad luck. I was just looking around really.' George slid the snow globe back on the shelf, glanced at the cuckoo clock high up on the wall. 'I should go. Nana Flo is probably looking for me.'

'You're still not allowed to talk to us, are you?' said Bobbie, crestfallen. 'I'm surprised you were even allowed to come here today.'

Saying goodbye is never easy, George, echoed George's father's voice in his head. *But a full farewell heals the heart faster.*

'Nice to see you both.' George slammed his teeth into his bottom lip as he bolted through the cabin door, leaving old Marley staring after him.

I need you to trust me, George. I know what's good for you.

Outside Gino's Cioccolata, Nana Flo was twirling on the heel of her boot. Her face lit up when she spotted him, her hair a halo of bright silver in the dark. 'There you are! I'm sorry I was a bit delayed, love. I ran into Martha from bridge, and I swear that vulture was wearing my new scarf. I left it behind last week.' She scowled, the fullness of her Irish lilt rearing up with her anger. 'That woman would steal the polish from my fingernails if I looked away long enough. Honestly, it's – Oh, Georgie, your eyes are all red. Have you been crying?'

'I just ripped my moustache off,' said George, steering her away from Marley's Christmas Curiosities. The air was thick with cloying sweetness, and it was suddenly making him feel queasy. 'Let's go home.'

'George! Wait!'

Nana Flo glanced over her shoulder. 'Ah,' she said, with dawning understanding. 'Do you want to see to that, love? I'll wait here for you.'

George waded back through a tide of bobble hats and frost-nipped cheeks. When Bobbie caught up to him, she stuck her hand out. The snow globe rested on her gloved palm. 'The old man wouldn't wrap it for me. He said he deals in "curiosities" not "frivolities". Apparently, there's a big difference.' She shrugged, looked at her boots. 'I only had £3.22 with me, but the man said that's exactly what it cost, so it seemed a bit like fate. Sorry about earlier. I know it's not your fault. Merry Christmas, George.'

George felt like he had swallowed a fist. 'Thanks,' he managed.

'You know, Mum and Dad are always saying they wish you'd come to ours for Christmas again. Just like it used to be. Why don't you?'

'We're staying home this year,' said George quickly. 'Thanks, though.'

Bobbie shrugged again. 'Tell your dad, anyway. And Nana Flo is welcome, too. Not Coco though. Doodle is terrified of her.'

George smiled. 'Yeah, I remember.'

'Do you, George?' she said quietly.

'BOBBIE HURRY UP I WANT FUDGE!' Clementine's voice barrelled across the fair, startling them from their conversation. Bobbie turned away before George could answer. He stared after his cousin. He caught sight of his aunt Alice then. She was standing with Clementine and Uncle Eli by the carousel, and looking at him with his mum's eyes. They were big and glassy, and her smile – George's mum's smile – was crooked.

The last time George had seen his aunt Alice, she'd been on crutches, her left leg wrapped in a cast that went past her knee, her face a mural of fresh scrapes. She couldn't look him in the eyes then. She just kept shaking her head, saying, *Sorry, sorry, sorry*, while George's father, stiff-backed and pale-faced, batted each one away. *Please let's not, Alice. Please, don't.*

The memory passed through him like a shudder, and George blinked himself back to the present. He realized Uncle Eli was cradling something in his arms – a bundle of blankets.

No – not a bundle. *A baby.*

A new *cousin*.

Alice raised her hand, but George was already turning from her, his throat full of half-formed words.

Certain people are better left in the past, George. They'll only remind us of what we've lost.

George's chest tightened as he moved through the crowds, away from his family.

On the bus home, George and his nan shed Christmas like a cloak, binning the last of their candy canes and dusting the powdered sugar from their hoods. With a heaving groan, the bus pulled away from the fair and at that precise moment, as if the magic of their wonderland adventure had finally sputtered out, Nana Flo's phone began to ring. The noise hung in the air like a siren, as Hugo Bishop's name filled the screen.

George shrank into his seat. Three long years had passed since his father first cancelled Christmas. Not just the tree, but the stockings and the presents too. The games and the turkey and the gravy and the carols and even the adverts on telly. They were not to speak of it any more. Not to each other, and not even to themselves.

Christmas is over, George, and it's not coming back.

There's nothing left to celebrate.

George tucked his hands into his pockets. In two days' time, Christmas would be upon them once more and his father's mood was as foul as ever. George brushed his fingers against his new snow globe, the last-minute miracle cool against his skin.

Old Marley's magic was beginning to stir.

Though he didn't know it yet, George was going to need every last drop.

2

The Scrooge in the Kitchen

When George and his nan arrived home, Hugo Bishop was sitting at the kitchen table, waiting for them. The lights were dim, the glow of the oven casting his face in shadow. With his black business suit, thick brows and pale complexion, he looked like a ghost, looming in the dark.

'And what time do you call this?'

George shuffled into the kitchen, his grandmother's hand warm on his shoulder. The afternoon, draped in tinsel and possibility, had completely galloped away from them. Now, the moon-faced clock on the wall said 9.07 p.m. 'Hi, Dad.'

'Sorry we're late home, Hugo. I *completely* lost track of time,' said Nana Flo airily. 'You know me, distractable as a squirrel. You haven't eaten without us, have you?'

'I ate at work.' George's dad gestured at the oven behind him, where a pizza was warming under the grill. The packaging was strewn across the countertop. 'Hawaiian Feast', it said in swooping red letters. 'Thought you both might like a treat,' he said, not quite looking at his son.

'Oh, a *frozen pizza*,' said Nana Flo brightly. 'How festive, Hugo.'

Summoned by new voices in the air, Coco wandered in from the living room and brushed against George's legs, as if to say, *Give me attention immediately*. George bent down to scratch behind her ears, while Nana Flo drifted over to the oven, humming to herself as she unearthed the pizza.

'*Mum*,' said George's father sternly.

She fell out of her song, tentative notes of 'We Wish You a Merry Christmas,' evaporating with the oven steam. 'Sorry, love. I didn't realize.'

She placed the pizza on the table, and George's father ran the wheel through it like a hatchet, as though he was trying to cut the plate underneath it, too. 'Got you one with extra pineapple, George,' he said as he pushed the plate towards him.

George rubbed his nose to keep it from wrinkling. 'Great . . .'

His father sat back then, satisfied. He began scrolling through his phone, the screen casting its reflection in his eyes. The refrigerator whirred; the clock on the wall ticked too loudly. As George plucked the pineapple from his pizza and tried, unsuccessfully, to feed it to an unimpressed Coco, he found himself wishing for the chaos of Marley's shop, the fizzing excitement of a carnival in motion.

'*Hmmph*,' said George's father, frowning at something on his phone.

Nana Flo turned up the dimmer on the wall, casting him in a sudden spotlight. 'How was your day, Hugo?' she asked pointedly. 'Did you get that problem sorted with the tenants at Pickwick Place? The one you were *yelling* about this morning at 6 a.m? I thought you had fallen down the loo.'

'It's to be expected around this time of year, Mum,' said George's father without looking up from his phone. 'People think they can delay their rent and blame it on the season. They must think I'm Santa Claus.' He slipped his hand into his pocket, took out a boiled sweet and began to suck noisily on it.

George's father was the owner of Bishop Estates. As a descendant of its founder, Walter Bishop, who was long dead, Hugo took his responsibilities as seriously as Coco took spying on their neighbour Mr Dubicki. In recent years, it had etched new lines in his forehead, and scattered the first strands of grey in his dark hair. George often wondered if these changes were really because his father was running a successful property-management company, or if it was the stress of trying to squeeze all those emails and phone calls and meetings into a hole in his life where they didn't fit.

'It's simple. If you haven't got enough money for rent, then don't go buying pointless presents no one will care about come January,' ranted George's father, the humbug bulging in his cheek.

'Sometimes a little festivity can brighten the whole year ahead,' Nana Flo said, tucking a stray curl behind her ear. 'Sure, when I was a girl, we barely had two pennies to rub together. I can still remember my father's leaky roof back in Dublin. All the pots we'd have to set out just to catch the rainwater. But we still made an effort to put a tree up, parcel away a present or two for –'

'*Mum.*' George's father flung an accusatory finger at her forehead. 'You know you shouldn't be wearing that.'

At the fair, the clip hadn't seemed remotely out of place, but suddenly, here, under the fluorescent lights of a kitchen where Christmas had been scrubbed from the countertops like grime, the bejewelled holly branch stuck out like a sore thumb.

Nana Flo slipped the clip from her hair, and blinked at it in surprise. 'Now, how on earth did that get there?'

'You know how I feel about that sort of thing,' said George's father gruffly.

Nana Flo turned the clip over in her hand. 'It's just a hairclip, Hugo. I've had it since I was a girl.'

George peered a little closer at the clip – the shining gemstones, the glittering edges. It looked brand new for something that must have been decades old.

'I know, Mum,' George's father said wearily. 'But can you please keep it in your jewellery box, like I asked? We don't do Christmas in this house. We agreed it was for the best.'

'*I* don't remember agreeing to anything,' grumbled George.

'Well, you were so upset back then, you would barely talk to anyone. It was up to me to make the right decision.' He looked pointedly at Nana Flo. 'For *all* of us.'

'Well, perhaps the time has come to reconsider that decision, Hugo,' she said carefully. 'We could spend tomorrow together, celebrate Christmas Eve as a family again. Build *new* traditions . . .'

George's father cracked the humbug between his teeth. 'We're fine the way we are, Mum.'

'We're not fine. We're frozen.' Nana Flo swept her hand around, at the blank walls, the silent house. 'For goodness' sake, love. A bit of Christmas spirit never killed anyone.'

George's father banged his fist against the table. The wood trembled, pizza crumbs leaping off the plate like they were trying to escape. Coco bolted under George's chair.

'It was *Christmas* that killed Greta, or have you *forgotten* that, Mum?' he burst out. 'Because for as long as I live I certainly won't, and neither will George, for that matter. He couldn't sleep for months afterwards. Or don't you remember?'

George's fingers were shaking, his bottom lip, too. There was a fire raging in his chest, and he wanted desperately to rip it out.

'Of course I remember, Hugo. It's the reason I moved in,' said Nana Flo calmly. 'And I'd much rather be here with both of you than back in that draughty old farmhouse, surrounded by memories of that awful day.' She blinked heavily. 'But it's been three years. We can't just shut ourselves off from –'

'And now you want to invite the spectre of that horrible Christmas back into our lives?' he snapped, as though he hadn't heard a single word. 'No. Absolutely not. I'll thank you to keep it out of this house and out of your hair for as long as you live here. And *that* is final.'

Nana Flo opened her mouth, then closed it again. There was a stretch of silence, George's father's breath whistling through his nose. She seemed to give up then, her shoulders slumping as she tucked the holly hairclip into the pocket of her cardigan. 'All right, Hugo.' She sighed. 'We'll do it your way.'

George's father swallowed. The moment had passed but it had left behind a dark shadow. It lingered over George, and perhaps it was a sudden shock of bravery, or the sight of his grandmother wilting like a flower beside him, but he decided, in that moment, he had had enough.

He pushed his chair away from the table. 'Don't shout at Nan. She's only trying to help.'

'Eat your dinner, George.'

'I'm not hungry.'

'You've only had one slice.'

'I *hate* pineapple pizza.' George scowled at his father. 'And I hate the way you're bossing Nan around.'

'That's enough, George. You know very well that Christmas is a trigger –'

'You're wrong!' George leapt to his feet, the chair clattering over. 'Christmas Eve might have been when Mum died, but it's not *Christmas* that killed her. It was *winter*. It was icy roads and bad snow and bad tyres and bad *luck*.'

'If she and Alice hadn't insisted on going to the shop to get that *bloody* marzipan –'

'Mum loved Christmas more than anyone. And when she was alive you loved it, too!' A sob thickened in George's throat. 'I think Nan can wear whatever hair thing she likes.

She can sing whatever songs she wants to. And – and – and –'
He sucked a breath through trembling lips. 'And if you don't
like it, then you're nothing but a – a – a – a SCROOGE!'

George's father stood up, but George was already turning
from him. He stormed out of the kitchen, Coco at his heels.
Over the determined thud of his footsteps, he could just
make out the bewilderment in his father's voice.

'What on *earth* is a Scrooge?'

'I believe it's an empty Christmas cracker, Hugo,' said
Nana Flo with a sigh. 'Something *utterly* and *completely* absent
of joy.'

'Oh,' said George's father, and before he could say anything
else at all, George slammed his bedroom door and pressed his
back against it.

He slid to the floor, the tears coming thick and fast down
his cheeks.

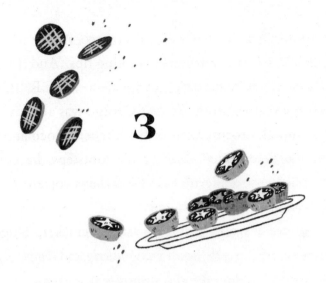

3

The Midnight Picnic

A short while later, there was a knock at George's bedroom door. George rolled to his feet as it creaked open, furiously scrubbing his cheeks with the back of his sleeve.

A dainty hand slipped through the crack, waving a white tea towel like a flag. 'I come in peace.'

'Do you also come with snacks?' George asked hopefully.

Nana Flo's head appeared round the frame in a frizz of silver curls. 'Of course,' she said, as though it was the most obvious thing in the world. Her eyes were bright behind her glasses, but the lines around them had deepened. 'You sound a bit stuffy, love. Are you feeling all right?'

'I'm fine,' said George, clearing the croak from his voice. 'I was just about to brush my teeth.'

'Oh, good. I'm just in time then.' Nana Flo slipped into the bedroom, holding a plate of oven-warmed mince pies.

George's stomach growled. 'How did you manage to sneak *those* past Dad?'

'You don't spend thirty years as an MI6 secret agent without learning a thing or two, George.'

'I thought you used to be a singing teacher.'

Nana Flo smirked. 'Did I . . .?' She shut the door with her bum. 'In any case, since you're now a witness to my contraband, I think the sensible thing would be to get rid of all the evidence. Don't you agree?'

George was already dragging his duvet on to the ground and heaping it with pillows. 'Way ahead of you,' he said, sinking to the floor.

They sat with their backs against George's bed, their legs kicked out like rag dolls'. The room was awash with colour. George and his mum had painted it together, choosing the brightest blue they could find for the walls, George holding on to the stepladder while his mother leaned back and covered the ceiling with the Milky Way.

Now the stars stretched over him every night, reminding him of her.

Nana Flo reached into her pocket and extracted six chocolate fingers.

'Don't say I never spoil you,' she said, adding the stowaway biscuits to their bounty. 'There should be more than enough sugar in here to get us through the night.'

George grinned around his mince pie, his cheeks stuffed like a hamster's. 'You know, as far as midnight picnics go, this one's not so terrible.'

'Ah, the feedback every grandmother wants to hear,' said Nana Flo dreamily. '*Not so terrible.*'

A noise from outside toppled the moment; there came the distant echo of footsteps stamping down the hallway, the sound of a door slamming. George took another bite of mince pie to hide his rush of disappointment. 'He should sleep through as much of Christmas as he can. He only makes it worse for everyone.'

Nana Flo smoothed a wayward strand above his ear. 'I'm sorry about your dad, Georgie. He shouldn't have taken his anger out on you tonight.'

'He shouldn't have taken it out on you either,' said George, a familiar spark of anger stiffening his spine. 'Why didn't you yell back at him?'

Nana Flo tipped her head back. 'I suppose because, despite your dad's age and my own along with it, he's still my boy, Georgie. And he's *hurting*. He's afraid to be reminded of your mum.' Her eyes misted. 'It's the desperate fear of it all. It can twist itself into anything just to find a way out. Anger, avoidance, carelessness.' She plucked a mince pie from the plate, turned it in her hand. 'A completely irrational disdain for Christmas.'

'So, he doesn't *really* hate Christmas?' said George, unconvinced.

'I think he hates what this season reminds him of,' said Nana Flo simply. 'But I suppose, in the end, it's all the same.'

'Yeah.' George rubbed the tightness from his chest, while Nana Flo rubbed his back in warm circles. Ever so slowly, the fist around his heart loosened, and he felt he could breathe again.

In the lingering silence, between the unmakings of a midnight feast, Nana Flo began to sing softly. Over the years of her life, her voice had brushed the rafters of school gyms and churches, concert halls and theatres. It had graced street corners and coffee shops, trad festivals, and, as an oft-repeated point of pride, every karaoke pub in Dublin and later, when she moved across the channel to start a life with George's grandfather, London. Even though her husband died when George's dad was a little boy, Nana Flo never stopped singing.

George could never quite understand how she managed to keep going. His bedside table was stuffed with old sketchbooks bursting at their seams, but he'd run out of ideas a long time ago. His art belonged, as most things seemed to, in the past. He had even drifted away from his friends at school, his weekends of football practice and trips to the arcade with Ben and Samir replaced by one-player marathons on his PS4 and reading graphic novels in his mum's favourite battered armchair in the attic.

When the song was over, the picnic was all but devoured. There was only a single chocolate finger left. George offered it to Nana Flo.

She snapped it in half, passed one piece back. 'For my co-conspirator.'

She climbed to her feet, pressing a kiss into the crown of his head. 'It won't always be like this, love. I promise.'

George desperately wanted to believe her.

'Where there's hope, there's always a little sprinkling of possibility.' Nana Flo smiled. 'In fact, I have a funny feeling Christmas will find its way back to us sooner than we think.' She stuck her hand into her pocket and presented Marley's snow globe to him. 'Which reminds me, I sneaked this out of your coat pocket earlier. I don't think there's any harm in stashing a little festivity in your room while you sleep.'

George took the snow globe gratefully. 'Thanks, Nan.'

She pottered into the darkness. 'Sweet dreams, George. May they be merry and bright.'

Well-fed and well-sung, George changed into his pyjamas and brushed his teeth. He was just drifting off to sleep when there came another knock at the door. This time, it didn't open. There was a gentle thud, a forehead pressed against the wood. 'I think this evening got away from us, George. From me. It's that time of year, I suppose. At least it will all be over in a few days.' His father's voice was so muffled, George had to strain to hear it. 'I hope you know I'm doing this for your own good. I just want you to be happy. To sleep well . . . You're probably asleep already, aren't you? Anyway, goodnight, son.'

In three long years, it was the closest Hugo Bishop had ever come to wishing his son a merry Christmas.

George turned over in bed, pulled his duvet up to his chin.

It was not nearly close enough.

The Insistent Snow Globe

George woke suddenly at 12.33 a.m. He opened his eyes to a mass of grey fur and a band of pressure stretching across his temples. Coco was asleep on his head again. He nudged her off and sat up. On the bedside table, Marley's snow globe was glowing. George examined the glass, confusion furrowing his brow. He hadn't expected it to be a night light, but here it was, bathing his bedroom in soft luminescence.

How strange.

He shrugged on his blue dressing gown and his grizzly-bear slippers, and took it with him.

The snow globe pressed against his pocket as he padded down the hallway, Coco swatting at it suspiciously as they went. Hugo Bishop's snores echoed after them, casting the vague air of a thunderstorm about the house. The rumble followed George all the way into the living room, where the curtains were open, spilling moonlight across the floor. The clouds had finally surrendered their bounty of snow, and were sprinkling Christmas over London like glitter.

George pressed his forehead against the window. He had lived at 7 Ebenezer Street for as long as he could remember, an orderly row of white-faced houses peering out over the same park. It had been decorated for the Christmas season, twinkling lights strung all along the iron-wrought railings. In the middle of the park, a towering evergreen had been lavished with red and gold baubles. Often, when George's father was late home from work and his nan was taken up with bridge or choir or one of her nebulous schemes, George would stand here a while and imagine that the tree belonged to him. That it was simply too big to fit in their living room.

Tonight, it looked like something out of a storybook. Despite the late hour, George spied a young couple wandering along the leafy pathways. Beside the duck pond, Mr Dubicki was reclining on a bench, his head tipped back to the starless sky. He was catching snowflakes on his tongue.

Coco, who had parked herself on the windowsill, mewled distrustfully at the sight.

The snow globe was warming in George's pocket. He plucked it free to find it even brighter than before. Frowning, he turned it upside down, searching for a switch.

There was none.

He peered in at the familiar snowman. It was all beginning to feel less like a coincidence, and more like . . . well, something else.

'I dream about you sometimes,' he whispered, drifting away from the world outside the window and into the one inside his head. 'The day we made you was the last time I heard my dad laugh.'

That night, George's mum had died and the sky fell down around him.

He sank on to the couch and Coco hopped up on his lap. George gazed into the globe.

'I wish Dad could remember what that day felt like.'

Coco pressed her paw against the snow globe, as if to say, *I wish that, too.*

Above the fireplace, a stately oil painting loomed over them. Walter Bishop, George's great-great-grandfather and founder of Bishop Estates, had occupied pride of place in the living room of 7 Ebenezer Street for as long as George could remember. He had been painted standing in a field beneath a giant oak tree, a hunting rifle slung artfully over his shoulder.

Along the rest of the walls, white squares marked the spots where his mother's art had once hung. Born so full of colour, it was no wonder Greta had become an illustrator. George's uncle Eli used to say that the Gierhart sisters could charm a cobra if they wanted, make a palace guard roar with laughter. Once, George's mother's work had cast personality across the house like a spell. Now, it was all up in the attic, packed away with old clothes and photographs, her favourite books, chair and jewellery.

A startled meow drew his attention back to the snow globe. It was shining out from George's fist like a miniature moon, so warm now he had to palm it from one hand to another, like a hot potato. The glass shook as it flew back and forth. The snow swirled around the smiling snowman, dusting his green hat with white flakes. The light flared, fierce and blinding, and then all at once blinked out.

George gasped. He turned the snow globe in his fist, then shook it again, but this time nothing happened.

Even so, he waited.

And waited.

'*Weird.*'

Coco arched her back, then hopped off the couch and trotted away, decidedly bored. Reluctantly, George tucked the globe back into the pocket of his dressing gown. He pulled the couch throw down and curled up underneath it.

Confusion soon gave way to exhaustion, George's lids growing heavy in the silence.

The pitter-patter of snow against the windowpane soon lulled him to sleep. He nodded off, unaware of the spell unravelling in the pocket of his dressing gown. While George dreamed of rolling fields and dancing snowmen, old Marley's magic leaked out of the snow globe in a tendril of silver smoke. It floated up over the fireplace and curled like a finger under the portrait's gilded frame. Coco watched with wide eyes as the air began to shimmer, the fabric of time and possibility shifting ever so slightly.

Somewhere in the snowy distance, a clock chimed 1 a.m.

And, in the living room of 7 Ebenezer Street, an oil-painted Walter Bishop reached up to straighten his tie.

5

A Most Unexpected Visitor

Approximately three and a half minutes later, George woke to the sound of grunting.

'Oi! You there!' said a booming voice. 'Bleary-eyed boy with the messy hair and drooling mouth. Yes, you. That's right. Wipe your chin. Look alive. I need some assistance, and *quickly*, if you don't mind.'

George shot up on the couch, blinking the dregs of sleep from his eyes. He looked around, searching for a figure in the dark. 'Dad? Is that you? I can't see you.'

'Up *here*, boy.' An impatient finger-snap. 'Follow my voice.'

George jerked his chin up to find a fully grown man crouching on the mantlepiece. His arm was flailing blindly in the dark. 'See now,' he said, waggling his fingers. 'That wasn't so hard, was it?'

George leapt off the couch. 'W-w-who are you?' he stammered, backing away. 'H-h-how did you get in here? I'm going to call the police!'

'How dare you!' The man's moustache twitched in offence. 'I've been here all along.'

The snow globe was white-hot in George's pocket. It pressed against his hip, reminding him of its presence . . . its *strangeness*.

It was then that he noticed the man's other arm was stuck *inside* the painting.

'No *way*.' He crept closer, taking in the rest of the crouched figure – the dark sweep of his hair, half hidden underneath a flat cap. The rifle dangling loosely from his shoulder. George gasped, like someone had pinched him. 'Hang on a minute . . .'

'I *am* hanging, boy! That's precisely the problem.'

'Are you Walter Bishop?' asked George, blinking just to be doubly sure. It was an impossible thing to ask, and yet the closer he crept, the more he saw. The man's face was strangely blurry up close. Even in the dimness, the texture looked less like skin and more like . . . well, paint.

'Well observed, Sherlock,' the man said impatiently. 'You don't have anyone else stashed in this painting, do you?'

George craned his neck. The painting was almost empty now; with Walter Bishop currently trapped like a fly in its frame, there was only his left arm and left boot left behind. George swore he felt a sudden breeze sweep over him, and when he blinked again the oak tree's leaves were rustling.

'This is so *weird*,' said George, rubbing his eyes to make sure he was really, *truly* awake. 'It doesn't make any sense.'

'What, the oil painting?' Walter huffed. 'As I *told* Maudie at the time, I *know* the painting is over the top. But in all honesty, if you can't commission an exquisite portrait of yourself in the prime of your life for future generations to marvel at when you're gone, then what is even the point of owning a tweed suit this fine? If it's good enough for Van Gogh then it's good enough for me. And at least I had the decency to pay someone else to do it. There's nothing more indulgent than a self-portrait.'

George was still battling his disbelief. 'No, I meant it doesn't make sense because you're . . . well, you're dead.' A pause, then his frown deepened. 'You've been dead for *ages*.'

'What's that got to do with anything?' demanded Walter Bishop. 'Enough whiffle-whaffle now, George, I think you'll agree I've been patient enough. You have exactly fifteen more seconds to process the wonder of what you're seeing. Then I need you to close your jaw up, march over here and put yourself to some use. Help me out of this blasted painting before I lose a finger. Or, worse, my good tie.'

They were interrupted by a shrill *meow*. Coco had crept out from behind the couch and was glaring at Walter Bishop with a level of disdain usually reserved for Henry the Hoover.

'And I'll thank *you* to mind your business, Whiskers,' he said, shooing her away. 'Since you do not have opposable thumbs, you are useless.'

George steeled himself and marched right up to the mantlepiece. 'Right. So you're coming out.'

'No, I'm going to stay here and do lunges,' said Walter drily. 'Stand still and square your shoulders.' He leaned out of the frame and placed his hand on George's shoulder, the force of it crushing George into the rug. 'Don't move. Or breathe, if you can help it.'

'Wait. What am I supposed to do with you once you're out here?' George was suddenly panicking at the thought of how his grumpy father would feel about coming face to face with his undead oil-painted great-grandfather.

Walter's moustache twitched in answer. It was as close to a shrug as he could manage in his present state. 'Not a forward planner, are you, George? You really should have thought of that before you summoned me.'

'I didn't summon you,' George protested. 'I was asleep!'

'So, if I was to inspect your pockets, I wouldn't find a magical artefact, then? A certain snow globe you may have shaken no less than three and a half minutes ago? Is that what you're telling me, *hmm*? Do you think I came down with the last rain shower?' Walter scooted out another inch, his rifle sliding down his arm and butting George squarely in the cheek.

'*Ouch!*'

'Careful, George. It seems gravity is against you.'

'Wait, you know about the snow globe,' said George with dawning alarm. 'Is *that* why you're here?'

He thought of what he had whispered to the snowman, and how, afterwards, the globe had flashed bright as a shooting star. *I wish Dad could remember what that day felt like.*

'Nice to see the Bishop intellect hard at work,' said Walter. 'Though I can see it's been somewhat diluted.'

George was too surprised and, perhaps, not *quite* brave enough to answer back. He looked confusedly at his ancestor, hovering inches from his face. He was real. He was *here*. And, yet, he smelt overwhelmingly of paint. 'How was I supposed to know what it was going to *do*?'

'Here's a piece of advice,' said Walter, as he yanked his left arm free from the frame. 'If you don't know what something does, don't repeatedly *shake* it. Now, stop pouting and give me your hands. My boot's wedged in tight, so I'm going to need you to pull with all your might. And move the hairball, unless you want a new rug for Christmas.'

Coco bolted across the room, fear sending her skittering underneath the bookcase.

'Clever, if mildly unlikeable,' said Walter appraisingly. 'I'm more of a horse person myself. Or a pygmy three-toed sloth if you can find one, but, of course, they're frightfully rare.'

George clasped both hands round his grandfather's wrist. Walter's skin was cool, and oddly coarse to the touch. He pulled with every ounce of his strength.

'*Heave*,' said Walter Bishop.

George heaved.

'*Heave.*'

And heaved.

'*Heave!*'

And *heaved*.

The frame creaked, the painting lifting off the wall.

'For goodness' sake, boy. Haven't you ever harvested a parsnip?' said Walter Bishop, his nose barely an inch from George's forehead now. 'Put your back into it.'

'I. *Am*,' George gritted out.

He heaved one last time, his muscles screaming, until *finally*, with a satisfying *creak!* and a resounding *oof!*, Walter Bishop came free of his oil painting and careened head first into George.

They toppled to the floor in a clatter of limbs. The frame, containing nothing now but the Devon countryside, swung back against the wall in a thunderclap, sending a shower of paint chippings down on top of them.

George covered his head with his hands, while Walter Bishop drew himself up to his full height and planted his hands firmly on his hips. 'Now, then. Where is your wayward father?'

As if summoned by the question, George's father came barrelling through the door to the living room. 'Who's there! Show yourself immediately!' he said, wildly swinging a golf club as he leapt across the threshold. 'I have a weapon and I'm not afraid to use it!'

Before George could get a word out, Walter Bishop swung his hunting rifle around and aimed it squarely at George's father's forehead. 'Well, now. That makes two of us.'

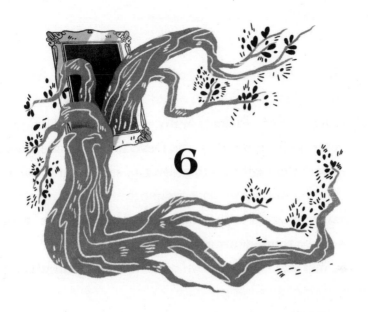

6

The Creeping Countryside

Hugo froze, his golf club hovering in mid-air. 'Who is that?'

George slammed his fist against the light-switch, and the room lit up in a shock of fluorescence. 'Walter, don't shoot! That's my dad!'

'Agh, my *eyes*!' cried Walter. 'For heaven's sake, use the dimmer, you blunderbuss!'

Hugo's golf club clattered to the floor. He glanced at the empty frame above the mantlepiece, then at Walter. His jaw unhinged, like a character in a cartoon. 'Is that . . . No. No, it *can't* be.'

Standing apart from each other in the living room at 7 Ebenezer Street, George marvelled at how similar his father and Walter Bishop looked. With strong chins, dark brows and deep-set blue eyes, they were almost like twins. Except, instead of an expensive tweed suit and matching flat cap, Hugo Bishop was wearing a stripy dressing gown and his hair was sticking up haphazardly above his ears. Thankfully, he lacked the thick moustache, too.

'Not bad for a ghost, eh?' said Walter proudly. 'I've managed to keep all of my hair.'

A strangled cry leapt from George's father. The colour drained from his face, until he was as pale as the white wall behind him. He flattened himself against it.

'In any case, I'm pleased to see you've come to your senses with regard to bludgeoning me, Hugo.' Walter dropped his rifle on the rug. 'Truth be told, the gun is empty. I'm a frightful shot. I just thought it would look classy for the painting.'

'George,' said George's father in a low voice. His eyes were trained on Walter, and he was being very careful not to blink. 'If you're real and not another figment of my imagination, I need you to go into the kitchen right now and call an ambulance.'

George stalked across the room. 'Of course I'm real. I'm right in front of you.'

'Wake your nan, too.' His father's lips were trembling now, a bead of perspiration sliding down his temple. 'Tell her I'm having a stress-induced hallucination.'

Walter snorted. 'For heaven's sake, Hugo. Don't be such a skitterbrook.'

'It's *talking* to me,' Hugo hissed. 'It's wearing the face of my great-grandfather and calling me names, George.'

George swallowed the dryness in his throat, and tried to push aside the fear that he had accidentally brought something terrible into their home. He slipped his hand into his pocket, the gentle warmth of Marley's snow globe reminding him of impossibility at work. He had little choice now but to put his trust in it.

'It's all right, Dad,' he said as reassuringly as he could manage. 'I don't think he's going to hurt us.'

Walter slipped his hand into his suit jacket and pulled out a gold pocket watch. 'All right, *your* fifteen seconds is up. We really must be going.'

'Going where?' asked George.

George's father stiffened. 'You are not going *anywhere* with my son.'

Walter crooked his finger at the picture over the fireplace, as though it was a dog being called to heel. 'Care to put a wager on that?'

There was a deafening *creak!*

For a heartbeat, George swore the ceiling was cleaving in two, but when he whipped his head round, he was even more alarmed to find the oak tree pressing its trunk against the empty painting, like it was trying to peer in at them.

Blades of grass were curling over the frame like fingers. There were only a few at first, tentative and searching as they brushed against the mantlepiece, but then the painting seemed to grow impatient. The frame trembled, the oak tree shoved aside as the entire field rose up like a giant snake, stones and roots and worms and clumps of earth dangling from its underside. It flung itself at the living room, hopped clean over the frame, and careened towards the floor in an endless green carpet that swallowed everything in sight.

'Watch out, Dad!' George lunged to steady the teetering bookcase before it flattened them both.

The painting belched, and a crooked tree branch punched its way through. It cracked the frame as it crawled out of it, more trees crowding in its wake. Leaves and twigs slipped through in twists and tangles, and birds chirped as they glided their way in.

The realization was as startling as it was unavoidable. The Devon countryside was creeping into their living room, and there was nothing George or his father could do about it. Hugo Bishop plucked his golf club from the floor and began swinging wildly. 'Back, back, back!' he yelled, the branches ducking and weaving around him. 'You won't take us without a fight!'

George, for his part, wasn't fighting at all. In fact, he was staring slack-jawed at the bullfinch chirping on the mantlepiece, the bushy-tailed squirrel currently storing his acorns in their fireplace. Even Coco was too alarmed to try to eat it.

'Not bad, is it?' said Walter, who had come to stand beside George. 'A little bit of magic goes a long way.'

George's father was still swinging and hacking. 'Not in my house!' he yelled, bringing the golf club down on a hawthorn shrub like a guillotine. 'Take that, you petal-faced monster!'

Walter sighed. 'This isn't his finest hour.'

The leaves kept coming, knitting themselves into heaving canopies as they tumbled through the frame and flooded the living room. George couldn't see the couch any more. When he wasn't looking, a tree had crept up behind him and taken the place of the bookcase. The floor was a thicket of wild grass, the blades tickling George's ankles as he hurried towards his father, who was, at that very moment, facing off with a quivering baby deer.

'You think you can traipse through my living room in the middle of the night with those innocent brown eyes, do you? *Hmm*?' Hugo Bishop clapped his club off the palm of his hand threateningly. 'Well, let me tell you something, Bambi. What you're doing right now is *trespassing*, and I can and *will* have you arrested for it.'

'Oh, good grief,' muttered Walter.

George wrestled the golf club from his father. 'Leave the baby deer alone, Dad. Just breathe, yeah? *Breathe.*'

George's father took a deep breath. It whistled through his nose, filled the barrel of his chest. Everyone stood very still. 'The moment may have got away from me.'

'Just a bit,' said George.

'You made quite the fool of yourself,' said Walter.

Hugo closed his eyes. 'I think I'm going to pass out.'

George looked at Walter, standing in the grassy remains of what was once their living room. 'What do we do now?'

Walter's eyes glittered. 'Well, George, this is your miracle.' He gestured behind him at the picture frame still spilling over the mantlepiece. 'You can either meet it head on.' He pointed to the living-room door. 'Or you can turn your back on it and pray it doesn't catch up to you.'

George looked at his father's bloodless cheeks. 'I didn't want to scare him,' he said quietly. 'I just wanted him to *remember.*'

'So, *show* him,' said Walter, a challenge in his voice as he pointed at the cracked picture frame. 'Great change requires courage, boy. It requires *action.*'

'You're right.' George grabbed his father's hand, turned his face to the fireplace. Before fear could catch him by the heels, he charged towards it.

'George!' shouted his father, stumbling after him. 'ARE YOU MAD?'

'Probably!' yelled George, but it was far too late to do anything about that now. The picture frame was growing bigger and bigger, the Devon countryside glistening emerald green inside it. The fireplace collapsed, the bricks rearranging themselves into steps that carried George all the way up to the mantlepiece. Still dragging his unwilling father behind him, he took a deep breath and flung himself into the frame.

The Marley in the Mirror

The painting stretched around them like a bubble. Time slowed, the world blurring to messy streaks of green and blue and white. George's ears filled with a peculiar ringing, his heart somersaulting in his chest as he freewheeled through the air.

And then, as quickly as it disappeared, the world snapped back into place. George's ears popped. He landed on the grass with a *thud!*, his father crashing down behind him. They lay still for a long time, their legs twisted beneath them, their cheeks pressed to the earth.

When George and his father finally lumbered to their feet, they were a world away from the living room at 7 Ebenezer Street. A bright blue sky stretched out in every direction, the sun shining fierce and golden in its centre. The hills rolled on, and the grass went with it, dotted by wildflowers and leafy trees, busy squirrels hurrying in and out between them. Dandelion kisses drifted lazily through the air. George caught one in his fist to make sure it was real.

'Dad, *look*.'

'Oh, I'm *looking*, George.' George's father was looking so hard, his left eye was twitching. '*What on earth* did you just *do*?'

'He found his courage and took a stand. Isn't that positively exhilarating?' Walter Bishop wandered past, beckoning to them to follow. 'Come along, Bishops, there's much to see. And, Hugo, try not to arrest any woodland creatures while you're here, won't you? It's terribly uncouth.'

George hung back, until his father fell into step with him. The collar of Hugo's pyjama shirt was ripped and he had lost a slipper somewhere in the commotion.

'Are you all right, Dad?'

'No, George. I am not all right,' he said stiffly. 'I'm either having a very elaborate dream or I've died in my sleep.'

'You're not dead.'

His father glanced at him. 'How do you know for sure?'

'Because I'm not dead, either.' George pointed to his father's feet. 'And, if this was heaven, you'd have both your slippers on.'

George's father skidded to a sudden stop. 'George,' he said, with a fresh wave of horror. 'What if this is *hell*?'

'Don't be absurd,' called Walter Bishop over his shoulder. 'I'm the best man I've ever known. What on earth would *I* be doing in hell?'

George cleared his throat awkwardly. 'Also, er, why would I be there?'

'What's to say I'm not hallucinating you?'

George shrugged. 'Well, you might be. We might *both* be. But I think we may as well try to enjoy it, while it's happening. What other choice is there?'

'*Excellent* logic, George.' Walter was leaning against a fence at the edge of the field now, waiting for them. 'You're a Bishop right down to your toes.'

'I'm a Gierhart, too,' said George quickly. 'Mum was always calm in the face of danger. She used to laugh on roller coasters – even the ones that go *backwards* – and she never screamed at spiders the way Dad does. And neither do I, by the way. Really, they're just anxious creatures. That's why they scuttle around so fast. I read that in a nature magazine once.'

Walter's moustache twitched in approval. 'You are a Gierhart right up to the hairs on your head, then. In fact, I'd wager that spirit is precisely how you got in here.'

'Bah!' Hugo slipped a humbug from the pocket of his dressing gown and popped it into his mouth. 'And what am I then?' he said, rattling it between his teeth. 'A no-good scaredy-cat, I suppose?'

Walter assessed Hugo with a short, sharp sigh. 'At this present moment in time, I'm afraid you, my boy, are a Scrooge.'

'There's that nonsense word again,' said George's father, fleetingly surrendering his well-heeled horror for a dollop of indignation. 'Why does everyone keep calling me a bloody *Scrooge*?'

'Most probably because you're acting like one,' said Walter, and George, walking between them now, said nothing.

Up ahead, an old farmhouse squatted in the valley of two humpbacked hills, its well-worn brick exterior peeking out between tentacles of ivy. Its thatched roof hung low over the windows, like a badly cut fringe.

'This is Nan's old house,' said George, quickening his footsteps. 'We used to come here for Christmas, until . . .'

'Belle Farm,' said George's father under his breath. 'What on earth are we doing back here?'

George narrowed his eyes as they drew closer. 'Hang on. I don't remember that old stable. And the door definitely isn't brown. Remember when Mum and I painted it bright yellow? Well, I don't think I was very helpful. A lot of the paint ended up on the doorstep, but she said it made it look like lots of little suns had dropped from the sky and . . .' George trailed off under the heat of his father's glare.

'This old house has been in the Bishop family for generations, George.' He stalled at the gate, then turned his suspicion on Walter. 'Just where exactly are you taking us?'

'I think you'll find it's a question of *when*, Hugo.'

The thick-necked chimney was piping silver smoke up into the air. George tracked it all the way into the sky, where the blue was getting paler and paler. Walter Bishop tipped his head back to watch it go, his moustache twitching *once, twice*. The sun disappeared behind a canopy of clouds, and a frigid wind cast winter's chill over them. When George looked around again, the trees were spindly and bare and a coat of frost glistened along the grass.

George's father tightened the belt of his dressing gown. 'Great. If the psychosis doesn't get me, the pneumonia certainly will.'

Walter clapped him on the back. 'We'd best be getting inside then,' he said, just as a wreath of holly popped out of thin air and hung itself on the front door.

'Look!' said George, who was not one bit cold despite the chill settling between his toes. 'It's Christmas here, too!'

Walter pushed the door open and strode over the threshold with the confidence of someone who could walk not just between seasons, but entire worlds, too. 'Let's see how many we can fit in, shall we?'

The house at Belle Farm was a maze of narrow hallways and poky rooms. It was rustic and ramshackle, everything slightly out of place and just a tad off colour. Walter led them towards the kitchen, where they squished shoulder to shoulder in the doorway.

'Can I interest anyone in a sprig of seasonal magic?' he asked, a smile curling beneath his moustache.

'Yes!' said George.

'Absolutely not,' said George's father at the same time.

Walter clicked his fingers.

The room blinked, then came to life. The kitchen was dripping in garlands and glitter, laughter mingling with Christmas carols that wafted from a tape recorder on the windowsill. There was a turkey crown roasting in the oven, along with a tray of potatoes and carrots. There was a boy standing in the middle of the kitchen. He was about ten or eleven, and was wearing a woolly brown jumper embroidered with a red-nosed reindeer. Beside him, a kind-faced woman with bright green eyes was fixing the hair sticking up above his ears. Her own had been swept away from her face by a familiar holly hairclip.

'That's Nan!' said George excitedly.

'And me.' George's father frowned at his younger self.

'Can they *see* us?' whispered George.

'Not unless they're highly observant and *exceedingly* special,' said Walter confidently. 'We're not here to give anyone a heart attack.' He glanced sidelong at Hugo. 'Just perhaps a change of heart.'

George's father ignored him. On the other side of the kitchen, his younger self was shimmying across the tiles, squawking along to the radio. Nana Flo joined him in dance, twirling the tea towel above her head like a flamenco dancer.

'You were quite the gigglemug back then, Hugo,' said Walter approvingly. 'Even after your father died, you and Flo always managed to make a joy of Christmas. In fact, it was your favourite time of the year.'

'I was a child,' said George's father, stony-faced. 'I didn't know any better.'

'On the contrary, you were wise beyond your years.' Walter raised his hands, pointer fingers extended like a conductor in an orchestra, and quickened the scene before their eyes. Christmas Day sped up, one blending seamlessly into another, and then another. George watched, slack-jawed, as young Hugo shed one paper crown for another, grew tall and gangly, sprouted spots and braces and an increasingly questionable parade of Christmas jumpers. Strands of silver threaded themselves through Nana Flo's hair, the same holly branch always fixed above her left ear. The berries winked at George, as if to say, *I see you*.

George anchored himself to his snow globe, shining sure as a sun in his pocket. It was the root of all this impossibility, and though he couldn't understand how it was happening, he knew well enough where, or rather, *who*, the magic had come from. George presented the snow globe to Walter as he conducted them through another Christmas at breakneck speed. 'You must know Marley, then? Did he send you to us?'

Walter Bishop regarded the orb with passing interest. 'Marley,' he said, pausing to tap his chin. 'Oblong head? Wire-framed spectacles? Ancient eyes haunted by an existence that contravenes the very fabric of time itself?'

'Err,' said George uncertainly.

'Propensity for the sale and barter of magical trinkets?'

'Yes!' said George. 'That's the one!'

'Never heard of him.'

'Oh, but —'

Walter gestured to the snow globe. 'Don't just bandy about your possessions, boy. Keep that tucked away in your pocket, before you drop it. I'm sure this Marley character, *whoever* he might be, and *wherever* you might have stumbled across his enchanted Christmas cabin, would be *quite* displeased to see you waving it about like that.'

Duly scolded, George slipped the snow globe back into his pocket. 'For someone who's never heard of Marley, seems like you know a lot about him.'

Walter shrugged, then turned his attention back to the kitchen. 'All I know is a shattered snow globe doesn't work. And that's science, not magic, boy.'

Hugo ducked his head round Walter. 'What on earth are you two blathering on about?' he demanded. 'And, more to the point, can we go home?'

'The terms and conditions of miracles,' said Walter. 'And no. Not until you remember how much Christmas used to mean to you.' He flicked his wrist and the world skidded to a sudden stop. 'Ah. Maybe this will jog your memory.'

Hugo, now a young man with straight teeth and stubble, was holding a serving dish heaped with Brussel sprouts. He set the dish down on the lace tablecloth, leaning over a young woman who, despite having not been there a moment before, was in the middle of telling a joke.

George gasped. '*Mum.*'

George sensed his father stiffen in the doorway, still and silent as a statue.

'. . . Because he had very low *elf*-esteem,' announced Greta, and both Hugo and Nana Flo collapsed into laughter.

'That was *awful*,' said Hugo, through a grin George hardly recognized.

Greta's eyes twinkled. 'The skill is in the telling of it.'

Hugo brandished a Christmas cracker across the table. 'Go on, then,' he said eagerly. 'Give us another.'

George's mum reached for it, and though George was on the other side of the table and two decades away on top of that, he flung his hand out to reach back. To his surprise, Nana Flo leaned over in her chair and patted his hand gently. George startled, but she was already turning away from him.

'Did you just *see* that?' he gasped.

'More trickery,' grumbled his father from the other side of Walter.

Walter only smirked. 'Well, isn't that something.'

Pop!

The cracker broke and a miniature trick mirror tumbled to the floor. A wedge of crêpe paper floated out after it. Hugo caught it in his fist and peeled it apart to find not one crown, but two.

'Oh, it's a twofer!' said Nana Flo excitedly. 'They're as rare as a purple reindeer!'

George blinked at his grandmother. 'Did she just –'

'I've had enough of this drivel!' George's father burst out suddenly. He sprang free of the door frame and stalked across the kitchen. The canvas of Marley's miracle stretched seamlessly around him as he kicked the back door open and disappeared into the garden without so much as a backwards glance.

'Look alive, George!' said Walter, hurrying after him. 'We've got a bolter on our hands!'

George desperately wanted to linger just one more moment, but Christmas was already dissolving around him. There was only the trick mirror left on the floor. He glanced at it as they passed, sure he had glimpsed a pair of ancient blue eyes watching him.

8

The Impossible Puddle

Out in the back garden, George's father was standing in the remains of a broken wreath, tapping his slipperless foot. Behind him, a veil of mist kissed the grass, turning the rolling countryside as pretty as a watercolour painting.

'Did you have a little tussle?' said Walter, gesturing at the crushed pine needles.

'It was an accident,' said George's father unconvincingly.

Walter stroked his chin, his eyes still on the wreath. 'There's a metaphor in there somewhere.'

'I don't want to see any more,' said George's father.

Walter rolled back on his heels. 'But we're almost there.'

'Almost *where*?'

The air shimmered, and out of it came George's mother's voice. 'Here, Hugo,' she said softly.

George and his father spun round, lightning fast. Greta was sitting on the garden bench, a woolly throw draped over her shoulders. She was holding out a dark green hat decorated with a silver bow. 'Merry Christmas, love. What do you think?'

Hugo was sitting next to her, every part of his body turned in as though she were a magnet. His cheeks were pink and his eyes were bright.

At the sight of his younger self, George's father deflated. 'Oh,' he said quietly.

'Well, I think it's very . . . *green*,' said the younger Hugo uncertainly.

'It's fashionable,' said Greta, fitting it on to his head. 'You look so handsome. So *daring*.'

Hugo sat a little straighter. 'Do I really?'

'Sometimes, a spark of colour makes all the difference in the world.' Greta grinned. 'Not that you needed much improvement.'

George's father turned his back on the moment. 'No,' he said, to Walter, to Christmas on the patio, to the magic knitting George's wish together. 'I'm done with this. Come on, George. We're going home.'

He took off, marching through the back door and across the kitchen at such a speed his dressing gown flew out behind him.

Walter and George followed him through the farmhouse, where Christmas had been turned off like a light-switch. Time was still moving about them, the air shimmering as they passed from one year to the next. When they reached the hallway, the front door was open, its wooden panels turned from brown to yellow. George stepped out on to the doorstep and found it suddenly splattered with paint.

His father was at the garden gate, tapping his bare foot. 'If we don't hurry, the rest of these awful Christmases will catch up to us.'

'Well, yes, Hugo, that's the idea,' said Walter, stalking outside. He squinted at the sky. 'Any minute now . . .'

Suddenly it started to snow. It was so thick and heavy George had to make a visor of his hand, just to see through it.

'Oh, great. Here comes the frostbite!' yelled his father, as they trudged back into the countryside. 'I think we came in from just up here somewhere. I recognize that oak tree! If we keep walking, we might get lucky and tumble back into the living room.'

The snow settled across the hills like a crust of icing. Soon it was deep enough for George's feet to disappear with each step. Walter, meanwhile, seemed almost to float on top of it, oil paint dripping from his sleeves and colouring the snow as he went. George was so distracted by the sight that he hardly noticed the snowman until it was right in front of him.

It smiled up at George with a crescent of turquoise beads. His left eye was a blue button.

'*Oh*,' said George, his heart lifting in his chest. '*There* you are.'

The air shimmered and a seven-year-old version of George appeared at his side, bundled up to his chin in a mustard pea coat and stripy green scarf. He pressed a button into the snowman's face, making another eye, as yellow as the sun.

'This is *so* strange,' said George, shuffling away from his younger self.

'Well, at least you're not melting,' said Walter, examining his hands with idle curiosity. They were starting to run. 'I suppose I've done my job. Your father certainly *remembers*, though I can't say he looks too happy about it.'

Behind them, George's father had descended into fully fledged panic. He was spinning on his heel searching wildly for an exit. '*Please* let us out,' he kept saying, over and over, but everywhere he looked, something else popped up instead.

Pop!

A plastic sled, turned on its side.

Pop!

A thermos of hot chocolate.

Pop!

A discarded woolly hat.

Pop!

The Hugo Bishop of three years ago, stalking across the field and twirling a forest green hat on the tip of his index finger. 'Told you I'd find it, love!'

Pop!

And George's mother, her sunflower hair sweeping down her back as she ran to meet him.

'I *adore* that hat,' she said, beaming. 'It makes you look like you can take on the world.'

Hugo proudly handed the scuffed hat to his son. 'Go on, Georgie. Why don't you do the honours? We'll have him ready just in time to greet your cousins.'

George watched his mother with wide, unblinking eyes as his younger self placed the hat on the snowman's head. There was a deep *pang* spreading in his chest.

The longer he basked in the shadow of his family's happiness, the further his father seemed to drift from it. He just spun and spun and spun, determined not to look. Determined not to feel.

'*Enough!*' he yelled at the snow, at the trees, at the sky. 'Let us out! *PLEASE!*'

When nothing happened, he marched over to Walter, his fists bunched by his sides. 'ENOUGH!' he shouted, right into Walter's face. Walter's moustache didn't even twitch. It did, however, begin to drip off his face. 'I want to go home!'

'Don't be such a spoilsport, Hugo. Stay a little longer,' said Walter. 'This was such a lovely afternoon, after all. It might do well for you to –'

'No!' snapped George's father. He flung his arm out, grasping for words. 'This *ridiculous* attempt to convince me of the merits of such a pointless, money-wasting, emotionally draining holiday is *pathetic* at best, and, and, and . . . *illegal* at worst!'

'Oh, codswallop!' said Walter, his tie falling on to the snow in blue splatters. 'You know this isn't just about Christmas, Hugo. It's about *life*.'

'And a new *attitude*,' said George, before he could stop himself. 'Christmas is a time of togetherness and happiness, and if you could just *remember* that –'

'I'm not talking to you, George,' said his father, a hand raised to cut him off. 'Christmas is gone. It is not coming back to 7 Ebenezer Street. You need to make your peace with that.'

George swallowed. 'But I just think –'

'*Enough*, George. You're just a child, for goodness' sake! It doesn't matter what you think.' He flushed then, the heat of the moment reddening his cheeks. He looked away guiltily.

George fell out of his argument. He backed away from his father, wounded. Being back at Belle Farm only reminded George of how much his father had changed. He was so different from the carefree, lovable father he had once been. The one whose eyes used to crinkle when he smiled, who used to sing off-key in the shower and overstuff his cheeks with popcorn on family movie nights until they all laughed so hard they lost their breath.

'And what about what Greta would think?' Walter inclined his head, to where George's mother was making the snowman's carrot nose.

Her name hung in the air like a thundercloud, swelling and swelling and *swelling*.

George's father's eyes flashed. When he spoke again, his words were dangerously quiet. 'Listen here, old man. I don't know where you came from or what you think you're playing at, but you're not really Walter Bishop. George and I don't need your fake wisdom or your half-baked life lessons. For heaven's sake, you're a bloody oil painting,' he hissed. 'And a *mediocre* one at that!'

'It's not Walter's fault,' said George, slipping the snow globe from his pocket and waving it in front of his father's face. '*I* wished for this. The snow globe is what brought us here. I thought it would help. I thought it would make you better.'

Hugo Bishop eyed the snow globe with distrust. 'I'm not sick, George.'

'Are you quite sure about that, Hugo?' Walter Bishop pressed a hand to his chest. It slid down the front of his jacket, and dripped on to the snow in noisy peach *splats!* His wedding ring landed in a fat gold drop, his hair following in a slick of black paint. 'Then again, what would I know?' said Walter, his eyes pooling into two blue splodges. 'I am only an oil painting.' His smile dissolved, taking the last of his words with it. 'And a mediocre one at that.'

'Wait, hang on a minute!' said George's father with alarm. 'You need to bring us back home first!'

But Walter Bishop had no voice with which to respond, his mouth lost somewhere in the puddle at George's feet. His eyes and nose were there, too, swirled with his tweed jacket and his good tie. George swallowed the whimper in his throat, as he peered at the oily remains of his ancestor. He felt, somehow, a small, hopeful part of him had melted, too.

The Accidental Avalanche

George's father shuddered. 'Well, that was . . . emotionally scarring.'

George tore his eyes from the snowy puddle. Over his father's shoulder, his family were having a snowball fight. Aunt Alice and Uncle Eli had arrived, and were joining in with yelps of delight. Bobbie and Clementine were there too, Clementine so small, the snow came up to her knees. They were all getting further away though, the field widening between them.

George turned the snow globe in his hand. 'That was pointless,' he muttered. Dad had remembered, but it hadn't changed anything.

His father swiped the globe from him. 'So, this is really how you've been making all this absurdity happen? Well, it stops here and now.'

He began to shake it violently.

'Be careful, Dad! Don't break it!'

'I know how a snow globe works, George. It's not rocket science. Now, stand back. I'm getting us out of here.' He wound his arm round and round, like he was about to pitch a baseball. 'It's getting warmer! I can feel it!'

George's mother's laughter was eclipsed by a distant rumbling. The ground began to tremble, the trees creaking as they shook the snow from their branches.

'*Dad*,' said George warningly.

'What?' he said, still shaking. 'Is it working?'

In the distance, on top of the tallest hill, a drift of snow had come loose and was sliding down the slope. 'No, but I think you might be making a bigger problem!'

Hugo glanced over his shoulder.

George snatched the snow globe back and stuffed it into his pocket, but it was already too late.

His younger self had disappeared. His parents, too. The snowman alone remained, his button eyes trained on the accidental avalanche as it thundered towards them.

George's father grabbed him by the shoulders and shoved him towards the nearest tree. 'Quickly,' he said, hoisting him on to a low-hanging branch. 'Get as high as you can and hold on tight. I'll be right behind you.'

George was halfway up the tree when he heard a high-pitched *meow!*

Coco darted out from a hollow in the bark.

George scrambled down after her. 'Coco!'

'Leave her, George! Our Coco is back at home!'

'But what if she's not? What if she followed us into the painting?'

George ducked out of his father's grasp and sprinted after his cat. Coco saw him coming, meowed one last time, then bolted straight into the path of the avalanche.

'Coco, NO!' George hurried after her, his slippers sticking and sliding in the snow.

'George, come back here!' George's father limped after him. 'You'll be flattened!'

In fact, they were all going to be flattened.

With a roar like a lion's, the avalanche reared up and leapt over the cat. George screamed as it crashed back down to earth, spitting chunks of grass and snow in its wake. And then it was upon him, too, the snow so dense and cold and blinding, George couldn't see the world beyond it, not the sun or the sky, or his father, shouting himself hoarse.

There was only the end of the world bearing down on him.

George shut his eyes and covered his head with his hands as the avalanche swallowed him whole.

10

A Matter of Deliberate Disbelief

When George opened his eyes, the world was dark and there was a feather in his mouth. He spat it out and began to dig himself free. It was much easier than he expected – and much warmer. The shift and crinkle of goose down alerted him to an unexpected change in his environment.

'George? Are you in there?'

The mound was ripped away. George's father's face appeared in the sudden dimness. His forehead was a cross-hatch of worry lines, the whites of his eyes wired in red. 'Oh, thank goodness.'

George blinked to find himself in his father's bed. They were sitting across from each other, half buried in his duvet. It was white as winter snow.

'What just happened?' said George in utter disbelief. 'I thought I was dead!'

There was an answering *mew* from underneath a nearby pillow. Coco peeked her head out, making sure it was safe. There were snowflakes matted in her fur. George brushed his hand through his hair to find a clump of his own.

His father was doing the very same thing. He squeezed his eyes shut, then shook his head, trying to knock the entire incident from his brain. When that didn't seem to work, he hopped out of bed and began pacing the room.

Coco jumped into George's lap, and both of them tracked his dad's movements as he marched back and forth, back and forth, muttering furiously to himself. He tightened his dressing gown as he went, slipped a humbug from his pocket and began sucking on it. He seemed to calm down then, remembered how to breathe – long and deep and slow.

When he turned on George, it was with clear eyes.

'You won't believe this, George,' he said, the humbug rattling between his teeth. 'But I've just had the most realistic nightmare.'

George gaped at his father.

'*You* were there, and *Coco* was there. And my great-grandfather Walter Bishop was there, too. Except he was an –'

'Oil painting,' George cut in.

'Yes,' said George's father, a note of surprise in his voice. 'And we were all back at –'

'Belle Farm,' said George. 'I know, Dad. It was real.'

George's father shook his head. 'No, no, no. It was a dream, George. You must have heard me shouting; that's why you're in here, isn't it? To check up on me. Well, don't worry. I'm fine.' He glanced at the clock on the bedside table. 'In fact, you can go back to bed. I have to get ready for work soon.'

'But it's Christmas *Eve*, Dad.'

'You know that doesn't mean anything.' His father shooed him away. 'The world still turns, and we must go along with it.'

'Dad, stop!' said George with rising desperation. 'It happened, and it was – well, it was sort of a miracle!'

George's father folded his arms. 'I'm not pretending anything. *You* are the one who's having *me* on.'

'There's a pine needle on your elbow.'

'What?'

'There.' George pointed at his father's left elbow. 'It's stuck to your dressing gown.'

George's father plucked the pine needle free, squinted at it. 'I probably brushed against a tree on the way home last night.'

'You drive to work.'

'Mr Dubicki's wreath, then.'

George snorted. 'You never call on Mr Dubicki. You think he's too cheerful, remember? And, anyway, you don't wear your dressing gown to work.'

George's father crushed the pine needle in his fist. 'Go back to bed. You must still be half dreaming.'

George swallowed the tremor in his voice, the sudden fear that perhaps he had imagined the whole thing, too. Maybe Marley's magic had tricked them both, and now Christmas was slipping through his fingers all over again.

But then – *no*. There was a prickle of warmth coming from his pocket. The magic *was* real – the wish just hadn't worked the way it was supposed to. It hadn't been enough to change his father.

George was simply going to have to try harder.

He took a steadying breath. 'I'll go back to bed and never mention any of this again, on one condition.'

His father raised his eyebrows.

'Tell me where your left slipper is.'

George's father looked at his feet, to find one of them bare. It was mucky around the edges, stray blades of grass sticking out between the toes.

He cleared his throat. 'It must have come loose while I was sleeping.'

George stood on the bed and lifted up the duvet, fanning it twice for good measure.

Nothing.

His father frowned. 'Well, it must be in my cupboard then. Where else would it be?'

George jumped off the bed with a determined *thud*. 'I think it's trapped in a past Christmas.'

'I told you not to talk about that kind of thing in this house, George.'

'What *thing*? Do you mean *Christmas*?' said George, his anger burning like a furnace in his chest. 'We just had *loads* of Christmases together, Dad. Don't you remember?'

Beep-beep, beep-beep, beep-beep.

'There's my alarm.' George's father rolled his shoulders back, a note of relief creeping into his voice. He gestured at the door. 'Go on then, back to bed.'

'*Fine.*' George turned from his father and stomped out of his bedroom. 'If you don't believe me, I'll just have to *prove* it!'

He marched down the hallway towards the living room. He kicked the door open like a hero in an action movie. It swung back on its hinges, clattering against the wall, and George bounded inside, expecting to find the guts of the Devon countryside splattered across the floor. 'Just look at –'

George fell out of his sentence.

He stepped into the room.

'Oh,' he said very quietly.

Then he said nothing at all.

The first brushstrokes of dawn cast a pallid light across the room. The furniture was perfectly in place, everything neat and proper as a doll's house. The fireplace was stacked and gleaming, the imposing oil painting of Walter Bishop hanging innocently above it. There wasn't a hint of shrubbery along the mantlepiece, nor a single grass stain marring the walls. Gone too were the insistent branches, the tuffets and hedges that had once jostled for entry. The oak tree had returned to its world, the ceiling had dropped back on to the house like a lid.

George cleared his throat. 'Maybe the magic is hiding,' he said, looking expectantly over his shoulder. 'If we just –'

The door frame was empty.

The distant hum of the shower alerted George to his father's whereabouts. He hadn't bothered to follow George into the living room. Instead, he had hopped straight into the bathroom to wash the night and its magic away. Soon he would emerge in his suit and tie, ready for work. They would fall back into their usual pattern, moving around each other like ghosts, George's mother's face looming in the back of their minds, her name swelling underneath their tongues.

Today was the anniversary of her death.

Now, it would pass in silence, and the following day along with it, and then Christmas would be over again for another year.

Coco, who had followed George into the living room, brushed her tail against his leg.

'Do you remember what happened, Coco?' he said. 'Or was it all just a weird dream?'

As if in answer, the cat trotted over to the couch and pawed at something underneath the throw. George whipped the blanket free to find his father's golf club glinting at him.

'I *knew* it,' he breathed.

The hairs on the back of his neck began to prickle. He snapped his head up to find himself suddenly rooted in the spotlight of Walter Bishop's gaze. There was something *different* about his portrait – something that could only be spotted at close range.

The dent beneath his brow had disappeared. The creases around his mouth had been smoothed away, the telltale etchings of a lifetime of frowns replaced by a subtly curling lip.

Walter Bishop was *smiling*.

George grinned. Their midnight adventure might not have worked last night, but Marley's magic was certainly real, and that meant there was still hope. After all, he was owed a last-minute miracle.

Of that, George was quite sure.

The Out-of-Place Man

Some hours later, long after Hugo Bishop had slipped from the house with the stealth of a burglar, George bundled into his winter coat and scarf, and set off for Ebenezer Park. The sun was gold and greedy, keeping all its warmth to itself. The clouds had splintered to reveal a crisp blue sky, the fallen snow now sloshing in puddles along the street.

As it happened, Nana Flo had business with the ducks of Ebenezer Park, so she accompanied her grandson on his outing. 'You're walking very fast,' she said, hurrying to keep up with George. 'Very *determinedly*, you might say.'

George hitched his notebook under his arm. 'I've got a lot of thinking to do today.'

'What sort of thinking?' asked Nana Flo curiously.

George opened his mouth, then closed it just as quickly. 'I'm not sure you'd believe me if I told you,' he said. 'So it's probably best that I don't just yet.'

'In your own time then, Georgie,' said Nana Flo mildly.

The wrought-iron gates creaked open and a rogue breeze slipped inside after them, rattling the holly bushes and shaking a handful of berries loose. George watched them scatter on the ground, and thought of Devon jamming its face through the gilded frame in their living room.

'Just remember you have your best schemer right here when you need her,' she added. 'I'm always happy to conspire at short notice.'

George glanced sidelong at his nan.

'Especially at Christmas,' she told him very seriously. 'In the meantime, I'll be over here with Bertha.' She patted the breadcrumbs in her pocket. 'She's the speckled one with the sassy waddle. A duck after my own heart, Georgie. Yelp if you need anything.'

She wandered away, and for a heartbeat George considered calling after her and telling her everything about last night.

Something stopped him, the snow globe suddenly like an anchor in his pocket. He thought of his father, bolting from the house that morning with his briefcase clutched tightly, while George begged him to come and look at the oil painting of Walter Bishop, just *once*. He didn't want to scare his nan off, too. At least not without cold, hard proof.

George sank on to the bench and listened to the baubles rustling in the wind. His nose was half frozen but he didn't much mind. He was tucked between the mighty branches of Christmas, and he felt all the better for it.

The park was mostly deserted, the residents of Ebenezer Street taken up with the hustle and bustle of Christmas Eve, last-minute shopping and incoming relatives giving way to an evening of board games and Christmas specials on the television. There was only Mr Dubicki out for his morning walk, and Mrs Kingsley reading a book beside the playground, while her daughter Amita played on the swings.

George slipped the snow globe from his pocket and shook it. He wanted another go. Another adventure, another chance at bringing Christmas home. The snowman smiled his turquoise smile, the snowflakes swaying lazily from one side to the other. But there was no warmth this time, not even the barest inkling of magic. Apart from the distant giggle of

Amita and a smattering of polite chit-chat between Nana Flo and Mr Dubicki, who had bumped into each other by the duck pond, everything was perfectly ordinary.

George frowned. 'Fine, then.'

He set the globe down on the bench beside him, rotating the snowman's button gaze until it looked out across the park. Then he turned his attention to his notebook, tapped the rubber end of his pencil against the page, thinking, *thinking* . . .

In the absence of Marley's magic, he would just have to make his own.

George set to work, losing himself in the flow of his drawing. Where once it had seemed impossible to put pencil to paper, now he couldn't seem to stop. He wasn't anywhere near as talented as his mum, but when he sketched the rest of the world melted away. He felt closer to her, somehow. He felt like he was sending a message, to himself and to her.

I won't forget you.

No matter what.

After a while, the bench creaked under the weight of a new visitor. George kept his eyes on his drawing, even as the ruffling pages of a newspaper disturbed the air beside his left ear. Instinctively, he grabbed his snow globe and settled it safely in his lap.

'Nice trinket,' came a man's voice from behind the newspaper.

George glanced up at him. 'Not really. It's broken.'

The man turned a page. 'Have you tried switching it on and off again?'

'It's a snow globe,' George told the brim of the man's grey hat, which was just visible over the very top of the newspaper. 'It doesn't *have* a switch.'

'Then how can it be broken?'

George frowned. 'It just is.'

The man *hmm*'d as he turned another page. 'Do you like cake?'

'Of course,' said George quickly. 'Who doesn't like cake?'

'Well, quite,' agreed the man. 'I was just thinking to myself that it takes more than one layer to make a particularly good cake. Wouldn't you agree?'

'I suppose,' said George slowly.

'Well,' said the man thoughtfully, 'perhaps it takes more than one good shake to make a miracle.'

George blinked in surprise. He was sure he hadn't mentioned anything about a miracle just now. *Had* he? 'What do you mean?' he said cautiously.

'I mean the next time you shake that thing, put some thought into it. Some *intention*. Then, see what happens.'

The man's response stunned George into momentary silence.

The man gave his newspaper a good ruffle. 'You know, I think they're quite alike in that way, in fact,' he went on. 'Cake and miracles. They're always well-received, they bring about a most pure form of joy, and, of course, they're both becoming increasingly gluten-free.'

George frowned. 'I think that last one is just cakes.'

'Ah, my mistake.'

It was then that George noticed the date on the man's newspaper. *1843*. 'Hey, you're –'

'Out of place entirely. You're quite right.' The man rose quickly to his feet and folded his newspaper in two. He jammed it under his arm. Beneath the shade of his unusually tall hat, George caught the telltale gleam of ice-blue eyes, the rim of wired spectacles balanced on the very tip of his nose. 'I must be off.'

George jumped up. 'Wait! It's you! I –'

'You don't mind if I leave a little Christmas behind, do you?' Marley reached into his pocket and hung a small white flake in the air, where it floated, quite impossibly, all on its own. He flicked it once, with his index finger. It began to twirl faster and faster and *faster*, and then –

It started to snow.

George tipped his head back just in time to see the sky release a fresh bounty, the flakes coming so quick and fast that he couldn't find the enchanted one among them. 'Woah!' he said, catching one on his tongue, just to see if it was real. 'It was dry just a second ago!'

'I suppose the sky had a change of heart.' Marley doffed his hat in farewell, then turned promptly on his heel, his parting words floating over his shoulder. 'You know, George, the only real barrier to magic is the limit of human imagination.'

And then he was gone, slipping through the gates and out on to the snowy street beyond.

'Wait!' George hopped up on to the bench and craned his neck over the hedge, only to find that old Marley had disappeared. There was no trace of his footsteps, the snow coming down so thickly that it had already crusted the pavements.

'Snowflake-catching, are you, Georgie?' Nana Flo was standing directly below him now. Her cheeks were pale and her eyelashes were brushed with snow, making her look like a friendly ice queen. 'You know, you could do that just as well from down here and you'd have considerably less chance of shattering your collarbone.'

'Did you see that tall man just now?' said George, still craning to see over the hedge. 'The one with the strange hat and the really old newspaper?'

'I'm afraid not, love. I was too busy gazing at my reflection in the pond.' Nana Flo held out a hand. 'Come on down before we turn into snowmen. I swear I can hear our kettle whistling my name.'

They ambled home in companionable silence, Nana Flo slowing every couple of feet to wish their neighbours a *Very Merry Christmas*. 'Best get it all out of our systems now,' she told George conspiratorially, before offering season's greetings to a nearby pigeon. 'Sometimes, if I'm feeling really rebellious, I do the lamp posts too.'

After a hot chocolate stuffed with marshmallows, and an afternoon of PlayStation, George was feeling much more like himself. He emerged from his bedroom just as the sun was setting, surprised to find it was still snowing outside. The fact that his father was at work on Christmas Eve was much less of a shock, but even so, it needled the spaces between George's ribs. Coco's arrival distracted him from this unpleasantness, the cat brushing against his ankles as if she could sense his loneliness.

George followed her down to the living room, where his nan was knitting on the couch.

'You know, Georgie, sometimes it really feels like there's magic all around us,' she said, tipping her head back to smile at him. 'Hard to spot, but easy to feel, like a pebble in your shoe. Does that sound a bit mad?'

George edged into the room. 'Actually, I don't think it sounds mad at all.'

Nana Flo set her knitting needles down. 'It's just that I've noticed the most peculiar change in old Walter Bishop's portrait,' she said, gesturing to the painting on the wall. 'After all these years of scowling off into the distance, he looks like he's *smiling*. See?'

George swallowed the sudden dryness in his throat. 'Yeah, I see it.'

'Oh, *good*.' Her shoulders slumped in relief. 'I thought I was imagining it.'

'Definitely not,' said George firmly.

Nana Flo *hmm*'d. 'If I didn't know any better, I'd say he climbed right out of that painting in the middle of the night and went traipsing on some impossible adventure and, when he climbed back into his portrait afterwards, he couldn't remember how to frown at all!' She laughed, for just a little too long. 'Can you *imagine*?'

'I can actually,' said George, the excitement of last night crowding on the back of his tongue. 'In fact –'

'But of course that would be impossible,' she cut in.

'Right,' said George, his heart sinking. 'There's no such thing as magic.'

'No. It would be *impossible*, because you would never go on an adventure without me.' Nana Flo's eyes glittered behind her spectacles, bright and green as the Devon countryside. 'Would you, George?'

George shook his head slowly. 'Not . . . on purpose.'

'That's what I thought.' She winked at him, and before George could make sense of what that wink meant, or just what precisely he was supposed to glean from it, she leapt to her feet and bustled into the kitchen. 'Now, keep an eye on the front door, while I crawl under the kitchen sink. I'm sure I hid my cinnamon stash in there somewhere, and I really don't see the harm in dumping a fistful or two into another hot chocolate. Do you?'

While his nan crawled through the kitchen cupboards like a mouse, George kept a wary eye on the front door, sure his father wouldn't come through it for hours yet. He would be buried in emails and phone calls and endless paperwork, anything to keep him from thinking about the magical avalanche that had rolled him home in the middle of the night.

After their mugs were washed and put away, George padded back to his bedroom to stash his snow globe underneath his pillow. Then he carefully removed his new drawings from his notebook and slid them in beside it.

Coco watched him from her precarious perch on top of the curtain rod.

'Tonight, I'm going to try our miracle again, Coco, and this time I'm not going to let Dad run away from it.'

It was George's solemn promise to himself, that, before dawn broke on Christmas morning, he would bring the spirit of the season back to 7 Ebenezer Street.

12

The Hopeless Child

George spent the evening curled up on the couch with his nose in a graphic novel. His nan kept him company, Coco studying the click-clack of her knitting needles with rapt attention. Every so often, Nana Flo would glance up to make sure Walter Bishop was still smiling in his oil painting, before smirking a little to herself.

Every so often, George would glance up, too.

He would breathe a quiet sigh of relief, and remind himself it was real.

It was real.

It is *real.*

Even so, the mood inside 7 Ebenezer Street was stagnant, the excitement of Christmas passing by their house as it rushed across the rest of London. George tried not to glance too often at the clock on the wall, wondering when his father would be home. Six o'clock came and went. George and his nan watched a silly quiz show in their pyjamas. 7 p.m. rolled around, with eight o'clock right on its heels, the small hand slowly inching towards nine. When their stomachs could stand it no longer, Nana Flo plated up their dinner, which was a wholly unfestive cottage pie, washed down with a glass of milk. A Wagon Wheel for dessert.

Afterwards, Nana Flo watched an old black-and-white movie called *Casablanca* while George watched the clock. At 10.58 p.m. on Christmas Eve, his father arrived home with a *grunt* and a *bang!* He stuck his head round the living room door, made eye contact with George for half a second before slinking back into the hallway. 'I'm off to bed,' he called out. 'I'll see you both in the morning.'

Nana Flo turned the television off. 'Hold on, Hugo! Your dinner's in the oven, and your *son* has been waiting up all night to see you.'

'I've already eaten,' came George's father's response through the walls. 'If I don't get to bed soon, I'll fall asleep on my feet.'

And then he was gone, shuttered away behind the battle lines of his bedroom door, avoiding the oil painting in the sitting room and the two very-much-alive Bishops frowning at each other underneath it.

Nana Flo sighed. 'Well.'

'It's fine.' George rolled on to his feet. 'I'm about to fall asleep, too.'

Nana Flo's face crumpled as she pulled him in for a hug. 'Oh, I'm sorry, Georgie,' she whispered, her breath warm against his ear. 'I really, *really* am.'

'You've got nothing to be sorry for,' said George, dutifully ignoring the crack in her voice. 'Merry Christmas, Nan.'

She pressed a kiss to his forehead. 'Merry Christmas, love.'

Ten minutes later, George tightened the rope on his dressing gown and stepped out into the hallway. The house was eerily quiet, the silence feathered by the padding of his footsteps and the nervous wheeze of his breath. A slant of light crept out from underneath his father's door.

'I knew you weren't really asleep,' muttered George. He knocked softly. 'Dad? Can I talk to you?'

An eternity seemed to pass, and then – 'Come in.'

George's father was sitting up in bed, scrolling through his phone. The reading lamp cast his face in shadow, making him seem much older.

George hovered by the nightstand.

'What is it, George?' His father set his phone down. 'You should be asleep. It's almost midnight.'

'I just wanted to give you something,' said George.

His father narrowed his eyes. 'We don't do presents in this house.'

'It's just a drawing. I did it in the park earlier.' George pulled a piece of paper from the pocket of his dressing gown and handed it to his father. 'It's of us. You, me and Mum. Do you remember our last Christmas together when we –'

'Yes, of course.' His father glanced at the piece of paper, noted the snowman wearing his favourite green hat. One corner of his mouth flickered, but only for a second. 'Thanks. Is that everything?'

George pulled another piece of paper from his pocket. 'There's this one, too.'

The silence was excruciating, George catching the precise moment when his father recognized his own startled face, charging head first into an avalanche. He blinked, then dropped the piece of paper like it was on fire. 'What a wild imagination you have, George.'

George levelled his father with a long, hard look. 'I know you remember what happened last night, Dad. Stop pretending.'

His father glared at him. 'Bed. Now.'

'No.'

'*George*. Don't test me.'

George crossed over to the window and threw the curtains open. The full moon bathed the bedroom in a wash of silvery light.

'What are you doing?' demanded his father.

George took the snow globe from his pocket, and held it between them like a bomb. 'Having another go.'

His father scrabbled to the edge of his bed. 'What are you going to do with that?'

'I'm going to shake it. With *intention*.' George raised his chin. 'I'm going to shake and shake and *shake* until my miracle works!'

And so he did.

His father lunged for the snow globe, but George leapt backwards. 'I want another go!' he shouted at the ceiling.

'George! Stop that!' His father whipped his head round, frantically searching for a rogue oil painting, or a houseplant that might find itself newly alive at any moment. 'The neighbours will think we've gone mad!'

'I want our world to be bigger,' said George as he shook.

The snow globe began to glow.

'George! I *mean* it!'

'I want our world to be brighter!' George's palm was warming quickly, the heat slipping into his bloodstream and racing towards his heart.

'Put that blasted thing down!' his father cried. 'Before you bring another awful curse down on us!'

Another awful curse, thought George, with a sliver of satisfaction. *I knew he remembered.*

'I want our world to be full of colour again!' he went on, feeling bolder now. 'Just like it was when Mum was alive!'

His father was jumping up and down, halfway to ripping his hair out. 'Stop this nonsense *at once*!'

'I want it to be full of the people who love us!' said George, the snow globe threatening to burn a hole in his palm. 'I want it to be full of the people *we* love!'

The snow globe flared – bright and white and blinding – before winking out completely. George dropped it on to the bed.

'There,' he said, suddenly breathless. 'It's done now.'

The silence stretched around them like a bubble, swelling and swelling and *swelling* and then –

Nothing.

A minute passed.

Another followed.

George's father relaxed his shoulders. 'Well, I suppose that puts the matter to rest.'

George was staring so hard his eyes were starting to prickle. 'Just *wait*,' he begged. '*Please*, Dad.'

'Wait for *what*, exactly?'

George spun round, straining for the barest whisper of magic, but there was only the tap dripping in the bathroom, his father tapping his foot on the carpet.

George's heart sank. 'The man lied.'

'What man?'

George shook his head. 'It doesn't matter. I just thought . . . I *hoped* something was going to happen. For a minute, it really felt like it was.'

'You're overstimulated,' said his father knowingly. 'You've worked yourself up with all of these fantasies and now you're upset. This is what happens to you. Remember? All this wishing and hoping doesn't do anyone any good.'

'But it's Christmas.' George slumped on to the bed. 'I just wanted it to go back to the way it was.'

'It will never go back, George. How can it?' His father sat down beside him, his hand firm on George's shoulder. 'We must accept reality for what it is and stop trying to change it. That way only madness lies. Try not to worry too much. Another twenty-four hours or so, and Christmas will be behind us again. Then we can go back to normal.'

Normal. The word pricked at George. There was nothing normal about their house, this strange, hollow place. It felt like a graveyard now, loneliness seeping like damp from its walls.

George swallowed. 'I don't want to be by myself tonight.'

His father sighed, pulled the blanket back. 'You can stay in here, then. Just for tonight. Just until . . .' he trailed off, but George heard the rest in his head.

Just until your mum's anniversary is over.

George stuck the snow globe in his pocket and curled up underneath the duvet. His father switched the reading lamp off and turned over, until they were back to back, both Bishops curling round their broken hearts. George soon fell into a deep sleep, lulled by the steady rumble of his father's snores.

Meanwhile, the snow globe glowed like a moon in his pocket, casting its secret spell.

13

The Elf on the Shelf

At 6.34 a.m. on Christmas morning, there was a knock at Hugo Bishop's bedroom door.

Ratatatat! Ratatatat!

Hugo turned over. His cheek was squished against his pillow, a line of drool striping his chin. Beside him, his son was smiling in his sleep. He was dreaming of a magical shop, and an old man with ice-blue eyes.

Ratatatat! Ratatatat!

The knocking grew louder, and despite the binds of his slumber, the younger Bishop began to stir. He cracked an eye open. 'D-dad?' he slurred. 'There's someone at the door.'

Ratatatat! Ratatatat!

The third knock was impatient *and* insistent. It was at this one that Hugo Bishop snapped his eyes open. 'What is that?' He flung his hand across the pillow and flicked the bedside lamp on. 'Who's knocking?' He stumbled to his feet and put his dressing gown on.

The bedroom door creaked open.

'Ahoy hoy?' came a small, tinny voice. 'Did someone order a miracle?'

George's father leapt up on to the mattress. 'Get up, George. Quickly!' he said, wobbling a little on his feet. 'There's an intruder!'

George's bleary eyes were trained on the swinging door, but he couldn't see anyone coming through it. He clambered up after his father, dimly aware of the heat flaring in his pocket. 'Dad, I don't –'

'*Shh!* I think we're being burgled.'

The door slammed shut, the reverberating *bang!* replaced by the pitter-patter of tiny footsteps. George and his father stared down, their eyes suddenly growing very wide.

There was an elf strolling across the floor. She appeared to be made of wood, and was wearing a stripy red-and-green onesie with a matching green hat. George recognized her from one of the shelves at Marley's Christmas Curiosities.

She paused to look up at them. 'Sorry I'm late. I was inanimate.'

George's father started screaming.

George, who was suddenly wide awake, grabbed him by the shoulders. 'Calm down, Dad. It's just the miracle. Sit down. *Breathe.*'

Hugo Bishop sank on to his pillow, his eyes still trained on the elf. 'What have you done, George?' he said with terror. 'My heart won't survive this. Not by a long shot.'

'Relax, Dad,' said George, sinking down after him. 'She's tiny.'

'I don't care. She shouldn't *be* here,' rasped George's father.

'Actually, I'm tall for my species,' the elf piped up.

'Which is . . .?' said George curiously.

'Festive puppetry.' They watched as she strolled all the way to the end of the bed, where she promptly began to climb his father's bookcase. She slipped several times, only to catch herself with her spindly arms at the last second.

'Don't. Mind. Me,' she huffed. 'I. Like. To. Sit. On. A. Shelf. Wheresoever. Possible.' She paused halfway up to catch her breath, grinned at them over her shoulder. 'And then, I just watch people for hours. Days. *Weeks*, if time allows. It's my very favourite thing to do.'

She resumed her climb, this time using her knobbly knees to shimmy towards the highest shelf. 'Come on, Tricksie. You can do this. Work *with* the shelf. *Think* like the shelf. *Become* the shelf. Concentrate. That's it. *Concentrate*.'

George's father scooted closer to him. 'George,' he hissed. 'If we make a run for –'

'No *way*,' George interrupted him.

The elf – or Tricksie, as she appeared to be called – swung a floppy leg over the top of the bookcase, and heaved herself up after it, her face grinding against the wood. 'That's going to hurt tomorrow,' she groaned. 'Might even need a new coat of varnish.'

'What if she murders us?' whispered George's father. 'Just *look* at that smile. It hasn't so much as *twitched*. Why does it have to be so wide, George? It's not natural.'

'Well, of course it's not natural. It's not supposed to be,' said George. 'And she's not going to murder us, Dad. She's made of wood. Plus, do you see a weapon anywhere?'

'She might have something in her hat, George.'

George rolled his eyes. 'She does not have something in her hat.'

'That reminds me,' said Tricksie, dangling her legs over the edge of the shelf. 'I have something in my hat.'

'AH!' bellowed George's father. 'I KNEW it, you creepy-faced cretin! Try anything and you'll be firewood by dawn.'

Tricksie looked at George. 'Is he *always* like this?'

'Unfortunately, yes,' said George.

Tricksie slipped her hat off and rummaged around inside it. 'I almost don't want to give you this now, but if I don't Marley will send me to the naughty corner, and I hate it there. You left this behind last night.' She pulled a large blue slipper out of her tiny green hat and fired it across the room with surprising force. It hit George's father in the face.

'Hey!' he shouted.

George trapped his laugh on his sleeve.

'I think the word you're looking for is *thanks*. I didn't *have* to go trekking through the Devon countryside looking for that, *especially* after how rudely you spoke to your first miracle-maker. We have *feelings*, you know.' Tricksie fixed her hat back on her head. 'Anyway. Now that that's done, we should probably get going.'

'To where?' said George, sitting up straighter.

'No,' said his father flatly. 'We are not going anywhere with you.'

'What if I say please?' said Tricksie sweetly.

'No.'

'All right, then,' she said, swinging her legs back and forth. 'What if I say, *Actually, Hugo, this is all just a formality, there's magic stronger than your foulest mood at work here and, as it happens, you have no choice in the matter of your impending adventure and will be coming with me, whether you like it or not?*'

George's father snorted. 'And how exactly does an elf no bigger than a baguette plan on bringing me *anywhere* against my will?'

Tricksie giggled into her tiny wooden hand. 'Oops, silly me. I knew there was something I forgot to mention. I brought a friend with me.'

'*Who* on earth –'

The rest of his question was lost in an almighty *crash!*

George whipped his head round just in time to see the bedroom door blow back on its hinges. The walls shuddered; the drawers rattled in their dresser. A hulking shadow filled up the door frame, strange branches of silver glinting at them in the duskiness.

George scrabbled backwards across the mattress.

Tricksie waved excitedly. 'Everyone, this is my close friend and personal confidant, Randolph. Randolph, this is George Bishop, requestor of the miracle. The man currently clinging to the bedpost is the subject of the miracle, George's father, Hugo. It looks like we have a mid-level Scrooge on our hands, but it's nothing we can't handle. Come on in and say hello!'

The shadow thundered through the doorway, taking half of it with him. He skidded to a stop at the edge of the bedframe and dipped his mammoth head in greeting. The tip of his silver antler nearly took George's eye out.

George's breath whooshed out of him. 'Is that – is he – it looks like – like –'

'It's a PURPLE REINDEER!' shouted his father, who was now pressed against his bedroom window, as far from the animal as he could possibly get. The bedside lamp spilled light across the room, illuminating Randolph in all his violet glory. 'GET AWAY FROM IT, SON, BEFORE IT EATS YOU!'

Tricksie clucked her tongue. 'Reindeers are herbivores, Hugo. Even I know that, and my head's hollow as a Christmas bauble. If he was *starving*, he *might* sample your curtains, but I wouldn't worry too much about that. He just ate your neighbour's Christmas wreath, so he's probably not hungry.'

Slowly, so as not to startle him, George scooted towards the reindeer. 'Hi, Randolph,' he said timidly. 'I like your antlers. They're really cool.'

Randolph blinked his big brown eyes, and huffed an appreciative breath through his snout.

'Does . . . does he speak?' George asked Tricksie.

'It's a *purple* reindeer. Isn't that impressive enough for you, George?'

'Does he *fly*?' asked Hugo, despite himself.

'Don't be *absurd*, Hugo. Reindeers can't fly.'

George frowned. 'Hang on a minute. What about Rud–'

'DON'T SAY IT!' yelled Tricksie.

'–olph,' finished George.

Randolph stamped his foot. The bedframe shook, and plaster fell from the walls like snowflakes. George's father whimpered into the curtains.

George looked around him, flummoxed. 'I just asked about –'

'DON'T MENTION THE R-WORD,' shouted Tricksie. She was jumping up and down now, flinging books off the shelf to get his attention. 'You'll only make him angry!'

It was much too late for that. Randolph grunted in offence, his hooves clopping pointedly as he turned round, leaving George face to face with his rear end.

'Sorry, Randolph,' said George. 'I've never met a purple reindeer before. I didn't know the R-word was a *bad* word.'

Tricksie sighed. 'It's not *strictly* a bad word. It's just that Randolph and *you-nose-who* are brothers. Estranged for years. Very hostile. It's a whole thing.' She waved her hand dismissively. 'I'd rather not get into it. For one thing, we don't have time, and, for another, it upsets Randolph.'

Randolph huffed in agreement.

George looked puzzled. 'So, I'm guessing you two don't work for Santa, then . . .?'

Tricksie snorted. 'Haven't you been paying attention? We work for *Marley*.' At George's confusion, she went on. 'Santa does *presents*. We deal in *curiosities*. Magical items – not just toys or books or puppies. Has to be regulated, as I'm sure you can imagine. Bureaucracy these days, eh?'

George stared at her. 'I'm confused.'

'Great.' Tricksie beamed. 'Let's get on with it, shall we? Randolph, over here, if you please.'

Randolph clopped over to the bookcase and positioned himself below Tricksie.

'OK, Bishops. Feast your eyes on this.' The elf tiptoed to the edge of the tallest shelf. She stretched her arms above her head, pressed her palms together and inhaled through non-existent nostrils. 'For Christmas and country!' she shouted, before swan-diving off the bookcase.

She hurtled through the air in a little green blur, missing Randolph by well over a foot and face-planting into the ground with an almighty *crunch!*

George yelped.

'How did she miss that?' muttered his father.

'*Ugh*, son of a *Krampus*,' said Tricksie, rolling herself over. She blinked up at them, her arms and legs splayed out like a starfish. Her smile was still eerily wide. 'I always forget I have terrible depth perception.'

'Are you OK?' said George, peering over her.

Tricksie leapt to her feet. 'Never better!'

Randolph bent his head and offered a silver antler to her. She held on tight as she was hoisted into the air, where she deftly swung round and positioned herself on the crown of his head. 'Okey-dokey, who wants to go next?'

'Neither of us,' said George's father quickly. 'There's no way I'm getting on that thing.'

George was already on his feet. 'I'll go next!'

His father shot up after him, catching the hood of George's dressing gown. 'You most certainly will not.'

Randolph blew a warning whistle through his snout. George's father raised his hands, backed up a little. 'Easy there, big fellow.'

George didn't waste his opportunity. He grabbed hold of a silver antler and kicked off the ground. With the help of Randolph, he was hoisted high up into the air, where he swung one leg over the reindeer's back and curled his fingers in Randolph's fur for balance. It was a deep violet, plush as a luxurious carpet and shimmering just a little. In that moment, George privately decided that a giant purple reindeer was much more impressive than one with a shiny red nose.

'George Bishop, get down here this second!'

Tricksie folded her arms as she peered at George's father. 'George can do what he likes. You're not his boss.'

'As his father and *legal guardian*, I think you'll find that I am.'

'Actually, tonight you are both officially under the stewardship of Marley.'

'What is that supposed to mean?'

'It means you're getting on this reindeer, Hugo.'

'Not unless you make me,' fumed George's father.

Tricksie looked at George. 'May I?'

George nodded. 'Definitely.'

With as much grace as the manoeuvre allowed, Randolph scooped George's father up by the belt loop in his dressing gown. He flailed blindly, spluttering and screaming, as he was flung into the air and on to the reindeer's back.

He landed in a disgruntled heap behind George. '*Ouch.*'

'Here,' said George, helping him to stretch his legs out. 'Just bend forward a bit to get your balance.'

'Let me off right this second,' his father demanded. 'This is kidnapping and it's against the law.'

Tricksie gasped. 'Do you mean Marley's law?'

'What? No, you little wood-headed imbecile! The *real* law. The one that governs *society*.'

'Oh, well, that's a relief.' Tricksie twirled on the heel of her boot and curled a hand round each antler. 'We don't answer to that one.'

Before George's father could respond, she threw her head back and yelled, 'GIDDY UP, RANDOLPH! FOR CHRISTMAS AND COUNTRY!'

'FOR CHRISTMAS AND COUNTRY!' cried George.

'I WILL SUE THE HAT OFF YOUR HEAD, TRICKSIE!' yelled George's father.

And then they were off, galloping through the broken doorway and out into the hallway, leaving all manner of disbelief far behind them.

The Obstruction in the Hallway

Less than five seconds later, Randolph skidded to a stop outside the bathroom. George crashed head first into the reindeer's neck. His father went nose first into his shoulder blade, both of them groaning from the sudden impact.

'This bloody thing should really have seat belts,' said George's father as he righted himself.

Hugo gingerly pressed his fingers against his nose to make sure it wasn't broken.

'*Weeeee-oooooo weeeee-oooooo weeeee-oooooo.*' Tricksie, meanwhile, was doing her best impression of a siren. 'Obstruction in the road! I repeat: OBSTRUCTION IN THE ROAD!'

She took her hat off, rummaged inside for a yellow hazard vest, then promptly shrugged it on. 'Nobody move,' she said, fastening the Velcro straps over her onesie. 'This could be a gremlin for all we know.'

George ducked his head round Randolph's antlers to find his nan standing in the middle of the hallway. Her hair was puffed up in rollers, and she was wearing her frilly pink nightgown. 'Well, well, well,' she said, a cup of tea clutched to her chest. 'What's all this, then?'

'Are you all right, Mum?' called George's father in a high-pitched voice. 'I can explain everything. Please, just try not to panic!'

'I'm not panicking, Hugo,' said Nana Flo calmly.

'Then call the police! These creatures have kidnapped us against our will!'

'Actually, I'm very willing,' said George.

Nana Flo's eyes twinkled. 'I can see why. It all looks like such fun.'

Tricksie glanced at George over her shoulder. 'I like this lady very much.'

'Nan loves adventures,' said George, remembering their conversation from yesterday evening. 'Can we bring her with us?'

'Great idea.' Tricksie turned back to Nana Flo and drew herself up to her full height, which was 12 ¼ inches (in shoes). 'Flower-headed lady,' she announced, in what George assumed was her most formal voice, 'we are about to embark on an adventure of positively *Christmas* proportions. Would you like to join us?'

'Where are you going?' said Nana Flo.

'It's a secret,' said Tricksie.

'All right, you've convinced me.' Nana Flo set her cup of tea down by the skirting board, and then pottered into her bedroom. 'I won't be a moment,' she called over her shoulder, and Tricksie, despite her earlier urgency, sat cross-legged on Randolph's head and waited for her.

'I thought we were in a rush,' said George's father pointedly.

Tricksie shrugged. 'Some adventurers are worth waiting for.'

'And some are worth kidnapping against their will, I suppose,' he said sourly.

Tricksie nodded. 'Precisely.'

'How can you tell the difference?' asked George.

'I am very wisdomous,' said the elf solemnly.

When Nana Flo emerged from her bedroom, her holly-branch hairclip was nestled snugly between two hair rollers. '*Splendid*,' said Tricksie approvingly. 'You've dressed for the occasion.'

Nana Flo flung her hands out. 'Don't just sit there gawping at me, boys. Help me up.'

With the help of Randolph, and the explicit refusal of his father, George managed to haul Nana Flo up on to the reindeer's back, where he helped her settle in the space directly behind him.

'Lady and gentleman and disgruntled Scrooge, prepare for take-off!' said Tricksie, stepping up to the antlers. 'Is everyone ready?'

'Yes!' said George.

'FOR THE LOVE OF GOD, NO!' shouted his father.

'Away we go!' whooped Nana Flo, kicking her legs in delight. 'FOR CHRISTMAS AND COUNTRY!'

Randolph took off at a thundering gallop, forgoing all conventional exits in favour of crashing straight through the wall at the end of the hallway, and leaping headlong into the street.

'ARE YOU INSANE?' cried George's father, as they landed on the footpath with an earth-shattering *thud!* The tarmac cracked beneath them, and the piercing shriek of three car alarms suddenly filled the air. 'WE COULD HAVE DIED!'

'But, crucially, you didn't,' said Tricksie brightly. 'All's well that begins well.'

'That's *not* how the saying goes.'

'I must say I quite enjoyed that little brush with death,' said Nana Flo, adjusting herself. 'It's been such a long time since I've seen my life flash before my eyes in a split second of sheer crippling terror.'

George, at that present moment, was too queasy to form words, so he concentrated on their surroundings instead. He found comfort in the traffic lights blinking from red to green, the chirp of a nearby robin, the moon fading from the sky. The puddles had almost disappeared, the last of the snow slowly melting away.

Randolph clopped in and out of them. The park twinkled under fairy lights, the trees swaying behind wrought-iron railings as they passed by. The sky blushed ballet pink, little faces appearing at faraway windows as the children of Ebenezer Street rose to greet Christmas at its dawn.

They soon left the familiarity of home behind them, galloping through winding side streets that spilled out into wide-necked roads. The city shirked brickwork in favour of chrome and concrete. Glass-faced shops huddled closer, Christmas orbs strung between them like shining gold planets. The air grew crisp around the edges, but George barely noticed the chill; he was too busy watching the world glitter.

The black cabs were already up and about, their amber lights winking at them as they streaked by. There were buses, too, each one red as a Christmas berry. George wondered what they would have looked like to the passengers if they could see them – three pyjama'd adventurers and one miniature elf riding a giant purple reindeer through the streets of London. Thankfully, Randolph slipped by, invisible, Marley's peculiar magic casting them in their own secret bubble.

The sun was peeking over the horizon, the final wisps of last night's clouds melting away. George spied the London Eye across the distant rooftops, watching over the city like a giant still snowflake. He could smell the river on the wind as they raced towards it. Nana Flo whooped in delight as they vaulted across Waterloo Bridge at such a speed their cheeks began to jiggle.

'Nearly there!' said Tricksie, taking a sharp right, and nearly flinging them all from the reindeer. George's father was concentrating so hard on the street signs, he was making himself dizzy.

'Where are we now?' he kept saying, over and over. 'This looks like Fleet Street, but I swear we just passed through it. If we could just slow down, I'd be able to read the –'

Nana Flo placed a gentle hand on his arm. 'Try to enjoy it, love. We'll get there when we get there.'

'Get *where*, though?'

'Well, exactly,' she said serenely. 'That's the fun of it.'

Tricksie steered Randolph down a narrow cobbled lane. She gestured at a bakery fringed in a purple candy-striped awning. 'There's Le Renne Violet,' she said excitedly. 'The owner, Celeste, was my very first miracle. Little girl with giant dimples. She's ninety-eight now, if you can believe it! Still makes the best croissants this side of the Thames!'

By the time George craned his neck to get a better look, the bakery was already gone.

'Wait a second,' Hugo piped up suddenly. 'I know that bakery. It's in East London. Right near . . . *Oh.*'

George suddenly stiffened in his seat. A strange, sickening feeling was pooling in the bottom of his stomach.

When he looked over his shoulder, the colour had drained from his father's face. 'Oh no,' he was saying under his breath. '*No, no, no.* Not here. *Anywhere* but here.'

When George turned back round, the cobbled lane had transformed into a leafy street. A familiar row of colourful houses unfurled before him like a rainbow. Tall and narrow, they wound up towards the sky like they were trying to pierce the clouds with their chimneys.

On this particular Christmas morning, they seemed to have done exactly that. Although it was crisp and dry across the rest of London, snow was falling on Cratchit Close – the street where the purple reindeer now roamed.

By sheer uncoincidence, it also happened to be the street where George's cousins lived.

A Highly Unusual Letter

Cratchit Close clustered round them, its kaleidoscopic houses all squished together like the bellows of an accordion. No. 63 was painted a brilliant sapphire blue, its arched windows peering out on to the street like watchful eyes. The front door was orange as a snowman's nose. Even from a distance, George could see the evergreen wreath hanging on it.

'So, what *exactly* is the plan here, Tricksie?' George's father shook the snowflakes from his hair. 'Do you think showing up on Alice and Eli's doorstep on a giant purple reindeer at the crack of dawn will cause anything but panic and chaos? Or are you aiming to traumatize their poor children for life, the way you have so readily traumatized *me*?'

Nana Flo rummaged in the pocket of her dressing gown and pulled out a Jaffa cake. 'Hugo, love, have a nibble of this and calm down,' she said, passing one over her shoulder. 'A well-timed carb never fails to put things in perspective.'

He batted it away. 'I mean it, Mum. This is George's mess. There's no need to drag anyone else into it.'

George eyed his cousins' house with mounting unease. He tried to swallow his doubt, but it was getting harder to stomach. 'Maybe this isn't such a good idea . . .'

Tricksie swung round, her face stricken. 'But I only ever have good ideas.'

'But what if we terrify them and ruin their Christmas?' said George anxiously. 'They've just had a new baby.'

'They have?' said his father, before catching himself. He cleared his throat gruffly. 'Well, precisely. We must think of the baby in all this.'

'What if the baby is why we're here?' reasoned Nana Flo. 'Is this what you wanted, Georgie? To meet your new cousin?'

George glanced at his father's stony face, the vein pulsing in his temple. He looked a million miles away from having a change of heart. 'I just don't know if this is the right kind of miracle . . .'

'HALT THE PARADE!' yelled Tricksie.

Randolph came to an abrupt stop, his hooves skidding on the icy street.

'There's been a terrible misunderstanding, Randolph. We must have an *immediate* audit, before this goes up the ladder to Marley.' Tricksie slipped off her hazard vest. She whipped her hat from her head and dropped the vest inside, before pulling out a tiny blazer and matching grey tie. She shrugged the blazer on, looped the tie round her neck and tightened the knot. 'Please bear with me, everyone. I'll try to make this as quick and painless as possible.'

She reached into her hat and pulled out a narrow piece of paper that went on and on and on. Then, a tiny pair of reading spectacles that were still much too big for her. After three attempts to settle them on her nose, she gave up. 'Oh, what does it matter,' she said, as she chucked them back into her hat. 'My eyes are made of ink.'

Randolph pawed the ground impatiently.

'OK, let's see here.' Tricksie scanned the piece of paper, as it unfurled past her shoes and on to the reindeer's head. He blew the end of it with his snout. '*I want our world to be bigger,* says George.' She stopped to look at George over the top of the paper, before changing her voice to a deep, grumpy baritone. '*George! I* mean *it!* That was you, Hugo.'

George's father scowled. 'You don't have to do the voice.'

'I like to fully commit,' said Tricksie.

She continued. '*I want our world to be brighter!* says George. *Put that blasted thing down! Before you bring another awful curse down on us!* That's you again, Hugo. Bit over the top, really. Everyone knows you can only purchase curses at Halloween. Anyway. George says, *I want our world to be full of colour again! Just like it was when Mum was alive!*'

Tricksie glanced meaningfully over her shoulder at the row of rainbow houses, before continuing, 'At this point, you began to jump up and down, Hugo. Then you said, *Stop this nonsense* at once! George, you didn't stop, and, may I say, good for you. Always stick to your guns. Instead, you said, *I want it to be full of the people who love us. I want it to be full of the people* we *love.* Now.' Tricksie cocked her head. 'This is the specific part of the wish. The colour bit, I admit, was vague. We could have gone to Legoland, and it would have been fine, but when you specified *love* – the kind that's both felt *and* received – well, the whole thing took a very definite shape. It became about family, and, unfortunately, that left little room for interpretation, and, believe me, I tried. Randolph and I *really* wanted to go to Legoland.'

Randolph whined longingly.

'I know, Randolph. It's not fair. It never is,' said Tricksie, patting him on the head. 'In any case, George, regarding your request, I'm afraid there was no righter destination than this one: 63 Cratchit Close, the home of your mother's sister and her family. Outside of the residents of 7 Ebenezer Street and a girl in your class called Sasha, these are the people who love you most in the whole world.' Tricksie lowered the paper, her smile stretching. 'And, happily, these are the people *you* love most in the world. It's really awkward when those two things don't match up.'

George's father folded his arms. 'That doesn't mean this isn't an awful idea.'

Tricksie rolled the paper up. 'Have I made a mistake, George?' she said nervously. 'Are you going to tell Marley? Please don't. I've only just come off probation for the accidental fireworks debacle of last year. How was I supposed to know you can't light them inside?' She shook her head mournfully. 'The truth is this is my favourite job in the whole world, and it's the only one I'm any good at.'

'*Are* you good at it?' said George's father sceptically.

Tricksie ignored him. 'I'll fix it,' she told George. 'If you don't want to see your cousins today, just say so.'

George brushed the snow from his lap, thinking. He could feel his father's glare on the back of his head. 'It's not that

I don't want to see them,' he admitted. In fact, he wanted to see them more than anything. 'It's just that Dad says –'

'This isn't your dad's wish, Georgie,' interrupted Nana Flo. 'You can make up your own mind.'

'And thank Marley for that!' Tricksie slipped out of her blazer and tie, balled them up and slam-dunked them into her hat. 'Otherwise we'd probably be at a calculator convention.'

'Oi!' said George's father.

'They won't be able to see us, right?' said George, glancing nervously at Nana Flo. He was sure she had reached out to pat his hand the night before at Belle Farm, but her expression was entirely serene now, and he thought perhaps he might have imagined it. He turned back to Tricksie. 'And they won't be able to see you and Randolph either?'

'Absolutely not,' said Tricksie confidently. 'Well. Probably not. Maybe. They'd have to be *very* special.'

'Right,' said George uneasily.

Tricksie nudged Randolph into a light canter. 'You see, George, some people are more observant than others when it comes to magic. On any given day, ninety-nine out of a hundred might look in our direction and see nothing at all, while one person might look at us and see absolutely everything, right down to the sparkly hairclip in Nana Flo's hair. I like to think of it as *Christmas roulette*.'

'How reassuring,' said Hugo sarcastically. 'Personally, I don't see how they *won't* notice us when your giant reindeer barrels through the front door and takes half of it with him.'

'Randolph can be very stealthy,' said Tricksie as she steered them up on to the footpath. 'He was top of his class in Clandestiny, four years in a row.'

'Do you mean Randolph went to *school*?' said George.

Randolph whined morosely, and George, for the first time, felt a sense of kinship with the reindeer.

'*Academy*,' said Nana Flo, completely out of the blue. 'I believe it's called the *Academy for Reindeers in the Festive Arts*. Or *ARFA*.'

George stared at her.

As soon as she said it, Randolph made that exact sound – *ARFA!* It was halfway between a bark and a sneeze.

'Well remembered!' said Tricksie approvingly. '*ARFA* is located right in the heart of the North Pole. *Very* prestigious. *So* expensive.' She pulled a ghoulish face. 'It deals in the four pillars of the Festive Arts: Clandestiny, Enchantment, Glamour and Entrepreneurship. If I may say, it has turned out some fine steeds in its time.'

Randolph wiggled his behind as he squeezed through the gate and into the front garden of 63 Cratchit Close. The snow had coated all the flowers in a shimmering silver dust. Without an ounce of hesitation, Randolph bent down and ate a fistful of primroses.

George's father slipped a humbug from his pocket and shoved it into his mouth. 'Pity they don't teach common courtesy.'

'Actually, they offer Common Courtesy as an elective.' Tricksie patted the reindeer encouragingly on the head as he went back for seconds. 'But Randolph took Art History instead. He loves Tintoretto.'

George was still looking at his nan. 'When did *you* learn about *ARFA*?' he asked curiously. 'I've never even heard of an academy for reindeers. I wouldn't have believed it even existed if I hadn't met Randolph tonight.'

Nana Flo looked past George as if she hadn't heard him. 'The front door is quite narrow, isn't it, Tricksie? How do we go about getting inside?'

Randolph clopped up the steps of 63 Cratchit Close, until his snout brushed against the brass knocker. It became suddenly clear to everyone that, even if the door was open, he was still too wide to squeeze through it, and yet Tricksie was tapping her chin in a way that implied she was considering it anyway.

'This is ridiculous,' moaned George's father. 'At this rate, you'd be better off posting us through the letter box.'

Tricksie lit up like a lantern. 'Hugo, you're a *genius*!'

The elf was already rummaging around in her hat. With a triumphant grin, she pulled out a small black square that looked not unlike an electronic car key.

'What is that?' said George, a touch uneasy.

'It's my shrinker!' she said delightedly. 'I completely forgot I had it with me. OK, everyone, deep breaths. Your lungs are about to get very small. Like me!'

'TRICKSIE!' yelled George's father. 'DON'T YOU DARE SHRINK ME or I swear – what's happening to my voice? Why has it gone all squeaky?'

The sensation of shrinking was a little bit like falling, only without the unpleasant *thud!* at the end. There was a lot of squeezing too, a tightness around the ears and the ribcage. All the air in George's lungs whooshed out of him until he felt shrivelled as a raisin. The world, meanwhile, got much bigger, like someone had inflated it. George marvelled at the winter flowers as they grew as tall as trees. The snowflakes floated down like lace tablecloths, while the front door shot up like a bright orange skyscraper.

'wow!' George wheezed. He sounded like he had inhaled an entire helium balloon, and the absurdity of his own voice in his ears made him giggle uncontrollably.

Nana Flo was giggling too. 'It sort of tickles, doesn't it?'

George's father's face was turning bright red. 'We better not come across any spiders!' he fumed.

'Don't worry, tiny Bishops. I'll protect you!' Tricksie had hopped off the reindeer at the very last second and was now standing next to them on the stoop, unshrunk and yet just a few inches taller. She pulled a big white envelope out of her hat and opened the triangular flap by Randolph's feet. 'Right then. Hop in! I'll mail you through.'

Randolph stepped into the envelope with the miniature Bishops on his back, and everything turned white.

16

Code Red

George Bishop had never mailed himself through a letter box before, so he had no idea what to expect. There was some light crumpling, a sudden shifting of gravity that made the bottom drop out of his stomach and then everything went sideways. He could feel the paper shifting against his cheek, heard Tricksie grunting somewhere on the other side as she heaved them up, up, up.

There was a long *squeak!* followed by a lot of scraping. Everything felt very tight all of a sudden, all of them sucking in a breath as they were shoved through the letter box. Then they were falling, down, down, *down* until –

Thud!

'*Ouch!*' they chorused, in perfect unison.

Even Randolph let out a disgruntled whine.

They were sideways again, their snuffling breath making the envelope feel suddenly very clammy. George listened for Tricksie as she clambered through the letter box after them. She managed to squeeze through with a few grunts and some choice swear words, before landing softly on the other side. The pitter-patter of her footsteps joined the smudge of her shadow as she peered at them. They were lifted from the floor, turned upside down and then unceremoniously shaken out of the envelope.

George was sure his face was bruised. And most of the rest of him, too. When Randolph righted himself, they quickly clambered back on. Now that they were tiny – not to mention trapped – there was safety in numbers.

'I can't feel my bum,' said Nana Flo as she shimmied into place between George and his father. 'I hope it's still there.'

'That was quite possibly the worst thing you could have done in the present situation,' announced George's father.

Tricksie loomed over them, her smile too near and too wide. 'Well, then you really shouldn't have suggested it.'

There was a noise from the other end of the hallway — the swing of a door, followed by the echo of approaching footsteps.

'Take cover!' yelled Tricksie, diving head first underneath the hall side table. Randolph galloped after her, the sound of his hooves like marbles rolling across the wood. They skidded out of sight just as George's aunt came striding down the hallway, the end of her bright red dressing gown swishing about her ankles. She stopped at the empty white envelope on the floor, and bent down to pick it up.

'*Oops*,' whispered Tricksie, peering out from behind a brass table leg.

'Where on earth did this come from?' murmured Aunt Alice. She opened the front door and stuck her head out. George craned his neck to get a better look at her. Her hair glowed golden in the morning light, the strands around her temples shot through with silver. She was bundled up in her dressing gown and slippers, and wearing stripy candy-cane earrings.

'What happened to my poor primroses?' She shook her head in disbelief. 'Must have been some gust. And *oh*. It's snowing. That wasn't in the forecast, was it?'

Something went taut in George's chest. There was so much of his mother in his aunt — the arch of her cheekbones, the dimple in her chin, her kind brown eyes. Even her voice carried the same cadence. It was amplified tenfold now, like she was speaking through a megaphone.

'Who's she talking to?' whispered Tricksie.

'Herself,' said Nana Flo. 'All the smart people do that. Sometimes I hold entire board meetings with myself.'

'My Greta used to do that.' George's father stiffened, as though the words had sneaked out of his mouth all by themselves.

Aunt Alice shut the door and pressed her back against it. She closed her eyes, her forehead crinkling. 'Is that you, G?' she whispered. A smile then, small and sad. 'If it is you, you're more than welcome. Always.'

The silence yawned, all five of them tucked underneath the hall table, waiting to exhale. Finally, Aunt Alice collected herself and drifted back into the kitchen, her slippers shuffling as she went.

Tricksie flopped dramatically against a table leg. '*Phew.* That was close.'

'What an adrenaline rush,' said Nana Flo delightedly. 'I haven't been this close to a heart attack since I jumped out of a Boeing P-8 Poseidon with only half a parachute.'

George's father said nothing. He just folded his arms and glowered at anyone brave enough to look at him. Still, it was hard for them to take him seriously while he was sitting on top of a miniature purple reindeer.

The door to the kitchen was ajar, Wham's 'Last Christmas' seeping out. They tiptoed towards it. 'Stealthily does it now,' said Tricksie in a low voice. 'No sudden movements or loud noises. We don't want the shrinker to wear off.'

'Could that happen?' said George with alarm.

Tricksie shrugged. 'Well, it's only a prototype.'

George's father dragged his hands along his face. 'It just keeps getting worse,' he groaned.

Christmas dinner was already well under way at 63 Cratchit Close. George spied a turkey browning inside the oven. The kitchen was small and narrow, but, in its colour and chaos, George saw more life than the entire house at 7 Ebenezer Street. He saw his mum, too. The bright yellow walls were adorned with her illustrations – hot-air balloons powered by magical sparks, musicians playing sunlight out of trumpets, and children, who looked just like George and Bobbie, sitting on the edge of the moon, fishing for planets. George swivelled his head back and forth, to try to drink it all in.

'Look at all that vibrant colour,' said Nana Flo admiringly. 'Doesn't it feel like the sun is shining on us?'

'Yeah,' said George wistfully.

Behind them, Hugo said nothing.

The kitchen fridge had become a scrapbook of Bobbie and Clementine's schoolwork and sticky love notes from Uncle Eli to Alice wedged between reminders about swimming practice and drama club. There were new photographs hanging on the walls: Clementine's first day at school, Bobbie's recent ballet performance, both girls holding a bundled-up baby outside a hospital and grinning from ear to ear.

There were old photographs, too.

'Oh, look, Georgie.' Nana Flo pointed up at the wall, to a snapshot of Alice and Greta when they were teenagers, squished cheek to cheek. They trotted on, past old snapshots of themselves. Family summer trips to Brighton, birthday parties, Christmases spent all together at Belle Farm. Though George was barely the size of a yoghurt pot now, he felt bigger here than he had in three long years. 'Mum is everywhere. *We're* everywhere.'

Tricksie looked at him over her shoulder. 'Are you surprised?'

George thought of his own house – the blank canvas that stood in place of a home, the white spaces where his mother should be. 'I . . . I thought they might forget about us.'

'Did you really?' said Tricksie, and, for the first time since George had met the plucky little elf, there was sadness in her voice. 'You know, when someone cares about you, truly and

137

deeply, they tuck that love away right down in the hard-to-reach place in their heart. That way, they have a way of holding on to you, even if you leave them.'

George was conscious of his father's silence over his shoulder. He couldn't bear to turn round and see the look on his face. Just in case it was blank.

The living room was wedged into a small conservatory at the back of the house. Through the glass double doors, George could make out the shape of Clementine. She was dancing. Her arms were swinging round and round, her curls flying across her face.

Tricksie nudged the glass-panelled door open just a crack. 'Let's see what's going on in here, then, shall we?'

They slipped inside.

The Christmas tree lorded over them, its baubles floating like shiny planets. There were pine needles strewn across the floor, each one tall and spiky as a sword. Garlands with red bows and silver bells had been strung above the windows and a row of colourful Christmas cards held court on the top of the bookshelf.

Tricksie gasped in excitement. '*Oh.*'

'Don't you dare sit on that shelf,' warned George's father.

Tricksie sat on her hands, rocking back and forth. 'Oooh, it's already so *difficult.*'

Clementine had stopped dancing and was now sprawled on the futon, catching her breath. She was wearing green velvet trousers, a sparkly jumper and matching glitter shoes. She kicked them over the armrest, her curls tossed across her face. Doodle was fast asleep on the floor, one golden paw blocking the morning sun from his eyes. His exhales swept over them in great warm gusts.

'He's *massive*,' said George, peering up at Doodle admiringly. 'Like a big furry giant!'

'And what if the big furry giant *eats* us?' said his father.

'Oh, he would never, Hugo,' said Nana Flo confidently. 'Just look how sweet they are together. I've missed those little faces.'

'Oh, what a *perfect* tree,' said Tricksie, who was sizing it up. 'It's so classy, isn't it?'

George and Nana Flo exchanged a look. The tree had amassed so much tinsel on its way up that it looked more silver than green, and was lavished with so many baubles that the branches drooped at the ends.

'Thanks!' said Clementine. 'I added more decorations when Mum and Dad went to sleep.'

'Did you really?' said Tricksie. 'Well, what an artistic talent you – Wait a minute.'

The elf gasped.

All of them turned their wide-eyed gazes on Clementine.

She brushed the hair from her face as she sat up, peering down at them with curious brown eyes. 'Hi, George. Hi, Nana Flo. Hi, Uncle Hugo. What are you doing down there?'

Tricksie tipped her head back and screamed, 'CODE RED!'

17

Not-So-Tiny Tim

Doodle woke with a jolt. He leapt to his feet, a bark trembling in his throat. George could see the years on him now – the shagginess of his fur, the white around his muzzle. 'It's OK, Doodle,' said Clementine soothingly. 'It's only magic.'

Doodle grumbled as he looked around. He sniffed the air suspiciously, but quickly settled back down again. It became clear that the dog couldn't see them. Only Clementine could. She hunkered down beside Tricksie. 'What's code red?'

Tricksie removed her hat and rummaged around inside it. 'Sorry about that. I scream when I get overexcited.' She pulled a giant candy cane out, and handed it up to Clementine. 'A Code Red is when a child spots you unexpectedly and must instantly be rewarded.'

Clementine's eyes lit up. 'I *love* candy canes,' she said, hanging it on her left ear.

George's father glowered up at his niece. 'For goodness' sake, Clementine, hasn't anyone ever told you not to take sweets from strangers?'

Clementine peered at him. 'She's not a stranger, Uncle Hugo. She's from Marley's shop. Just like my *Forever Flake*.' She pointed over her shoulder, to where the snow was still bucketing down. George squinted, but he couldn't find the imposter flake twirling in among the rest. 'At first, I put it in my bedroom and made a very big mess,' said Clementine sheepishly. 'Then I threw it out of my window and look!'

Clementine smiled, revealing the gap made by her missing front tooth. Then, without warning, she leapt to her feet and skidded from the room, like she was on fire. 'Wait here!'

The door swung back on its hinges, and beyond it they could hear the patter of her glittery shoes as she raced out into the hallway and up the stairs.

'This is getting more dangerous by the minute,' said George's father. He craned his neck, searching for Tricksie. 'Hey! Where did that blasted elf disappear to?'

'Over here!' Tricksie was sitting on top of the bookshelf, waving at them from between two Christmas cards. 'Sorry! I couldn't resist.'

'I suggest you get down right away and get us out of here, before Clementine comes back in here with Alice,' said George's father furiously. 'Or would you like to give her a heart attack? Truly, you should be in prison.'

Tricksie hopped off the shelf and landed in a clatter of limbs. 'Oh, Hugo,' she said, springing up and dusting herself off. 'There isn't a jail cell in the world that could hold me.'

Clementine returned, dragging her sister into the conservatory. Bobbie was holding a bundle of blankets in her arms, and walking very carefully.

'All right, Clem,' she said softly. 'What's the big surprise?'

Clementine pointed at Randolph and his stowaways.

Bobbie wrinkled her nose. 'What is it?' she said, confused.

'It's George,' announced Clementine. 'I told you he'd come.'

Bobbie looked at her little sister. 'George doesn't come here any more, Clem. Uncle Hugo doesn't let him. Remember?'

Clementine put her hands on her hips. 'Then how come he's here, too?'

Bobbie sighed, her voice turning stern. 'Clem, you told me there was an *emergency* downstairs.'

'There is!!' said Clementine, raising her voice.

'Shh!' scolded Bobbie. 'You'll wake the baby!'

The bundle of blankets began to stir.

'See.' Bobbie sank on to the couch, and began rocking the baby back and forth. 'You're not the youngest any more, Clem,' she chided. 'You're six now.'

Clementine's face crumpled. She scrunched her fists up and began to breathe very quickly, in and out *and in and out and in and out and in and out*.

'Uh oh, she's gonna blow,' said Tricksie.

'Clem, it's OK,' said George, waving up at her. 'Bobbie's not even supposed to see us. You can only see us because you're different. I think it's because you're special.'

Tricksie nodded. 'VERY.'

'Of course she's special,' said Nana Flo. 'And, by the way, there's never a good time to grow up, Clementine. Whether you're six or seventy-six, I don't recommend it.' She laid a warm hand on Hugo's shoulder. 'People only do it when they have to.'

'We're going now anyway, Clementine,' added George's father pointedly.

'No, don't go yet, Uncle Hugo!' cried Clementine. 'You haven't met Tim.' She pointed at the baby in Bobbie's arms, ignoring her sister's alarmed expression. 'He's *tiny*, isn't he?'

'Well, not to us,' said George. Tim was too far away for George to see his face, but he waved up at him anyway. 'Hello, Tim!'

Nana Flo and Tricksie waved, too. And Randolph tossed his head in salutation.

'Tim's blinking his eyes now,' said Clementine, studying her little brother. 'That means *nice to meet you.*'

'You're starting to freak me out, Clem,' said Bobbie uneasily. She pushed her glasses up her nose and leaned forward, narrowing her eyes as though trying to trace their shapes in the nothingness.

'You know, it's *almost* like she can see us,' remarked Nana Flo.

George could just about make out the baby's cheek now, the soft brown of his eyes, framed by curling lashes.

'He's got Mum's eyes,' he said, rising up to get a better look.

'Well, isn't he gorgeous!' cooed Nana Flo.

George's father was doing his best not to look at the baby. In fact, he was studying the spine of an atlas halfway down the bookcase. 'I want to go home now.'

'Are you OK, Uncle Hugo?' asked Clementine. 'You look like you've eaten a volcano.'

Tricksie regarded George's father with uncharacteristic concern. 'He does look a bit rosy-cheeked.'

'Hugo,' said Nana Flo softly. 'Why don't you say hello to the new baby?'

'I SAID NO!' bellowed George's father.

The room trembled. A bauble leapt from the tree and shattered across the floor. Bobbie pulled backwards with a gasp, cradling Tim to her chest. 'What was that?'

Clementine was about to reply when Randolph's right antler *popped!* back to full size.

Nana Flo screamed.

Tricksie leapt backwards. 'Uh oh, uh oh, uh oh.'

'The shrinker's wearing off!' cried George.

Randolph was top-heavy now. He tipped forward, Clementine catching him by the snout at the last minute. It *popped* back to full size and nearly headbutted her in the face. She scrabbled backwards with a loud yelp.

Doodle leapt in front of her and started barking.

Tim started wailing.

'Shhh!' Bobbie scolded the dog. 'Not you, too, Doodle!'

'Do something, Tricksie!' shouted George's father. 'Before you kill us all!'

Tricksie scooped the shrinker out of her hat and clicked it furiously, just as Randolph's hind legs began to inflate. 'No, no, no, no, no, no, no!'

The reindeer shrank back to miniature size at the exact moment the glass door swung open. It knocked Randolph across the floor and sent them all sliding underneath the tree just as George's aunt marched into the room. Tricksie was too slow to escape, so she played dead, flopping to the floor in a bundle of wooden limbs. Just in case.

Aunt Alice stepped over the elf without even noticing her. 'What on earth's going on in here?' she said, making a beeline for Tim.

Bobbie handed the baby to her mother. 'It was Clem. She got Doodle all riled up.'

'Well, where is she now?' asked Aunt Alice, turning on her heel. There was only Bobbie, looking around helplessly, and Doodle growling at the Christmas tree.

'Oh,' Bobbie said in a very small voice. 'I . . . I don't know.'

Clementine had completely disappeared.

The Accidental Shrinking

There was a faint giggling coming from behind George. He turned to find his cousin peering at him through the branches of the Christmas tree. Clementine was holding a pine needle in her hand. 'Look, George!' she said, swishing it back and forth. 'I'm tiny too!'

Out on the floor, Tricksie was still lying motionless. Her eyes had gone very wide.

'Uh oh,' said Nana Flo. 'Something tells me that wasn't supposed to happen.'

Clementine crept through the branches towards them. 'Can I get on the reindeer?'

'Absolutely not,' said George's father. 'You're not even supposed to be down here in the first place.'

George peeked up through the baubles and branches, to where Bobbie was staring blank-faced at the tree. 'She must have gone upstairs when I wasn't looking,' Bobbie said uncertainly. 'I was distracted with Tim.'

'Well, try to keep the noise down, love, please,' said Aunt Alice. 'I'm going to put Tim down for his nap. And could you keep an ear out for Dad? He should be home any minute.' She turned round, her foot knocking against Tricksie and sending her skidding across the floorboards. Then she slipped from the room and nudged the door closed behind her.

Bobbie leapt up from the couch and began scouring the room. 'Clementine?' she whispered nervously. 'Are . . . are you in here somewhere?' When there came no answer, she shook the thought away. 'No, I'm being silly.'

Doodle started sniffing around the tree.

Tricksie sat up in a flash, a wooden hand clapped against her cheek. 'OK, that was my bad.'

'You *think*?' shouted George's father. There was a vein bulging in his left temple, and his cheeks were turning a concerning shade of puce. 'YOU SHRANK CLEMENTINE!'

'I LOVE it!' said Clementine, as she hurried out from under the tree. 'Everything is so *big* from down here! I can see up Bobbie's nose!'

'She's fine, see?' said Nana Flo, trying to calm the situation.

'She's not fine. Her sister can't see her any more!' boomed George's father. 'If you don't unshrink Clementine right this second, Tricksie, I swear I will have you fired and sued and THROWN IN PRISON AND –'

The room began to tremble.

'Stop yelling! You'll break the shrinker again!' cried Tricksie, but it was already too late.

Randolph's rear end *popped* back to full size. They all slid towards the reindeer's head, grappling for purchase amid a desert of violet fur. Nana Flo crashed into George's shoulder, and yelped as her legs inflated. George's lungs ballooned in his chest, and the air came rushing back in with an audible *wheeze*. For a heartbeat, he thought he might float away, but Nana Flo grabbed hold of his dressing gown and anchored him to the reindeer, until the rest of him caught up. Somewhere over George's shoulder, his father was yelping at his fingers, seven of which had grown big and thick as sausages.

'I'm all bent out OF **SHAPE!**' he yelled as his head inflated.

Nana Flo turned round. 'For goodness' sake, Hugo, KEEP your VOICE **DOWN. OH DEAR, MY HEAD'S GONE HUGE AGAIN!**'

Randolph's antlers sprang up with an audible *pop!* He keeled over into the Christmas tree and sent a shower of baubles crashing to the floor. Clementine, who expanded all in one go, stood up to find herself stuck between the branches and covered in reams of tinsel. She caught a bauble in mid-air, and batted another one out of the way before it could bop George in the face.

She erupted in giggles as she climbed out of the tree. 'This is the best Christmas ever!'

Bobbie, who was across the room with a cowering Doodle, burst into hiccoughing shock. 'You're back!' she half shrieked. 'Where did you disappear to? I couldn't see you anywhere!'

'I'm magic!' said Clementine, swishing the end of her tinsel around.

George, now returned to full height, felt around for his nose and ears, and was relieved to find they had grown just the right amount. His dad had settled back into himself and was scrabbling around in his pockets for a humbug, while Nana Flo was readjusting the holly clip in her hair.

'Wow,' said George in breathless disbelief. 'That was . . .'

'Fun?' said Tricksie hopefully.

'Horrendous,' said George's father.

'Delightful,' said Nana Flo.

George settled on: 'Unexpected.'

Bobbie shoved her glasses up her nose. 'So is George really here?' she asked her sister, while looking around the room.

'Yep. *And* he's on a purple reindeer.' Clementine splayed her arms. 'A *huge* one!'

'Which is not without its complications . . .' said Nana Flo uneasily.

Tricksie frowned. 'Tell me about it. Old Scroogey-face over there broke my shrinker.'

'I didn't even touch it!' protested George's father.

'You didn't have to,' Tricksie scolded him. 'Your bad attitude did all the work for you. I told you the magic was temperamental. A bit like *you*, actually.'

'*Shh!*' said George suddenly. 'Do you hear that?'

It was the sound of the front door closing. Uncle Eli's voice wafted in from the hallway. 'I'm *home*! And I brought the custard!'

Clementine gasped. 'Dad's home!'

'Oh no!' said Bobbie. Panic rushed in all at once. The Christmas tree was broken, the floor was a mess, Doodle was restless and both girls were utterly dishevelled. And yet, all things considered, the chaos paled in comparison to the giant purple reindeer currently standing in the middle of the conservatory, chewing on a full branch of pine needles.

George spied Uncle Eli through the doors. He was still wearing his hospital scrubs, and his hair was frizzing around his temples. There were circles under his eyes but his smile was toothy and wide. 'Oi, where is everyone?'

'We have to get out now,' hissed Tricksie. 'I can't risk another code violation!'

'He's coming this way!' said Bobbie urgently. 'We need to distract him!'

'I'll do it!' said Clementine, springing into action.

'Good plan,' said Tricksie. 'How are you going –'

Before she could finish, Clementine barrelled through the double doors, her arms flung out like a human airplane. 'AAAAAAAAAAAAAAAAAAAHHHHHHHHHHHH! IT'S AN EMERGENCEEEEEEEEEEEEEE!' she screamed, whipping past her father and sprinting out into the hallway, where she thundered upstairs. Uncle Eli spun on his heel and ran after her, laughing. 'Clem!'

Upstairs, Baby Tim started wailing.

'OK, that works,' said Tricksie, nudging Randolph through the door. 'Let's hurry.'

They left Bobbie behind them, in a mass of broken Christmas baubles, and crept into the kitchen. At full size, the act of sneaking was much more difficult. Tricksie steered them round the table, while Randolph tried his best not to knock anything over. The table was already set, wooden place mats and sparkly green napkins arranged around mismatched plates and frosted glasses. There was a Christmas cracker at every place, with a name written under each one.

'Look!' said George, pointing to his own name as they passed it. 'There's a space at the table for me!'

'Oh, goodness. And for me!' said Nana Flo, squinting at the one next to it. On the other side, Hugo's name was scrawled in Bobbie's handwriting, too.

'How did they know we'd be coming here today?' asked George.

'They didn't,' said Tricksie. 'They set these places every year, just in case you change your mind.' She glanced at George's father's bowed head, then sighed.

When they opened the front door, a rogue breeze swept inside, bringing a flurry of Clementine's snow with it.

'It'll be a tight squeeze,' said Nana Flo, tucking her legs in front of her. 'I suggest we all scrunch up.'

'Remember your *ARFA* training, Randolph,' said Tricksie, as Randolph stepped up to the door frame. 'We want a nice quiet exit. Subtle as a bee's sneeze.'

Randolph squeezed into the door frame, his legs straining as he pushed, and pushed, and *pushed*. Finally, with a creak and a *whoosh!* the frame buckled and then spat them out into the garden. The house trembled, the hall mirror falling from its perch and shattering across the floor.

Somewhere upstairs, Aunt Alice's voice rang out. 'What is going on down there? Is that Doodle again?'

George flinched, as they hurried into the garden. 'We've ruined their house!'

'Don't worry about that!' said Tricksie, waving her hand in dismissal. 'It's all covered under Marley's Insurance Policy!'

Bobbie rushed out after them in her socks. She craned her neck, directing her gaze at the nearest street lamp. 'If you're really out there, I just want you to know that I miss you,' she called out. 'If it was up to me, you could come by any time. Properly. With as many purple reindeers as you like.' Her smile wobbled. 'Merry Christmas, George.'

'Merry Christmas, Bobbie,' said George longingly. And then they were off again, streaking across Cratchit Close and leaving all the joy and possibility of Christmas far behind them.

The Case of the Secure Stocking™

By the time the reindeer turned out of Cratchit Close, it had stopped snowing. Now there was only the glum clip-clop of Randolph's hooves as they wandered down winding streets that all looked the same. Perhaps it was George's imagination, but the reindeer's fur seemed duller now. It was less of a bright purple and more a drab maroon.

Tricksie was unusually quiet. Every so often, she would look over her shoulder at George's father and sigh dramatically.

'There must be a quicker way home than this,' he grumbled, when they had bustled down their tenth street in as many minutes. The London Eye was peering at them over the distant rooftops, but they didn't seem to be getting any closer to it. Hugo knocked his knees against Randolph's hide to spur him on. 'You were going at the speed of light on the way over here, and now you're walking like we're in a funeral procession.'

'Maybe we are,' said Nana Flo morosely.

'What's that supposed to mean?'

Tricksie spun round, her little eyes flashing. 'IT MEANS YOU KILLED CHRISTMAS, HUGO!' she exploded. '*Holy Grinch toenails*, read the room! We're miserable.'

George's father folded his arms. 'You're the one who brought us on this absurd outing.'

Tricksie balled her wooden fists. 'You are so *difficult*.'

Randolph huffed in agreement.

'Why?' challenged George's father. 'Because I'm against vandalism and trespassing?'

'Because you're breaking your son's heart!' Tricksie brandished her wooden hand at George's forehead. George shrank in his seat. 'I haven't seen a child so sad since the time Randolph and I accidentally trampled a little girl's train set and then blew up her bedroom. Goodness, I've never *met* a Scrooge so set in his ways and I've been at this job so long,

I've had nine hip replacements. How many wishes will it take for you to wake up and see your son's happiness is more important than your own stubbornness?'

Tricksie's explosion sucked the last of the warmth from the air. The wind was crisp and biting; George could feel it in his bones.

George's father glared at Tricksie. If looks could kill, she would have dropped dead, but she simply turned round with a *hmmph*, and steered them on their way. They crossed the river in silence this time.

The world soon began to look familiar to George. The roads grew narrower, the buildings smaller. Corner shops and restaurants hunched shoulder to shoulder beneath strings of fairy lights. George spied his favourite Chinese takeaway, opening for business. It was right next to a three-storey bookshop called Great Expectations, where Nana Flo brought him every Friday after school. It was past 11 a.m. now. There were more people milling about, but of course nobody noticed them.

When they trotted past The Busy Bean, a coffee shop just a stone's throw from Ebenezer Street, George's father sat up straight.

'Nearly there,' he said, with great relief. 'Just so you are aware, Tricksie, I will be filing a restraining order against you the second I get a chance. You are not to come near my family ever again. Especially my son.'

'Or *what*?' said Tricksie, glaring at him over her shoulder.

'Or I'll have a word with your superior. *Marley*.'

'Marley would *never* take a meeting with you,' said Tricksie, but there was a note of doubt in her voice.

'He will if I say so,' said George's father. 'In fact, I'm going to –'

Brrrring brrrring!

Brrrring brrrring!

'What is that?' he said, looking around him. 'Is that someone's phone?'

Randolph came to an abrupt stop.

'Well, don't look at me.' Nana Flo patted the pockets of her dressing gown.

'*Santa wept*. This is so embarrassing. I thought I put it on silent.' Tricksie slipped her hat off and pulled out a human-sized mobile phone. She glanced at the screen. 'It's my cousin Moxie. I better take this,' she said, waving at them to be quiet as she pressed her entire face against it.

'Tricksie speaking. Yes. Are you sure?' She gasped. '*Son of a Krampus*, you're *kidding*. *Now?* Is he breathing? Sure. Well, that's good. I did say they could be tampered with, didn't I? No, no, I'm not playing the blame game. But if I *was* playing it, you'd be the one to blame. No, I know. It's not about that. But it is, a little bit. Yes, I understand.'

'How long is this going to take?' whispered George's father, who, despite his disdain for the elf, had retained a simmering respect for work phone calls.

'Shhh,' said Nana Flo. 'I'm trying to eavesdrop.'

'Yes, I'll tell him now. He's here with me. A bit maroon, but it's been a long one,' said Tricksie. 'Very high-level Scrooge.' She glanced at George's father, then quickly turned away. '*Awful*. Remember the Grinch? *Worse*. I swear.' A chuckle. '*Honestly*. I completely lost my temper, and you *know* how professional I usually am. I *know*. But *this* guy is something else.'

'We can all hear you,' said George's father flatly. 'Wrap it up.'

'Yeah, that was him. I *told* you. OK, I better go. I'll get right on that. Great. Speak soon. Bye bye, bye bye bye. OK bye.'

Tricksie dropped the phone into her hat, then settled it back on her head. 'Sorry about that. *Big* emergency with a Secure Stocking™ up in Glasgow. I'm afraid it's got all the markers of a classic Clausnapping.'

'A what?' said George and his nan in unison.

'A little girl has got Santa trapped inside a Secure Stocking™,' Tricksie explained. 'She's demanding a ransom. The whole works.'

'Kids these days are *so* wily,' said Nana Flo approvingly.

'What's the ransom?' asked George.

'Oh, just the usual. Four puppies, a talking unicorn and a pair of Taylor Swift tickets. Which is of course ridiculous. Those tickets are impossible to get.'

'What's a Secure Stocking™?' asked Nana Flo. 'Sounds like I could do with a pair. Mine are always falling down.'

Tricksie chuckled. 'A Secure Stocking™ is a stocking designed with special face recognition so your brothers and sisters can't peek at your presents first. They're one of our most popular items. Anyhow, the girl in question somehow managed to turn her Secure Stocking™ into a Catch 'em Claus, which were outlawed in the late 90s. And she's got Santa trapped inside it right now. Which means we have to go to Glasgow.'

'Goodness,' said Nana Flo. 'When?'

'Ideally? Ten minutes ago.'

Randolph made a strange barking noise.

Tricksie sighed. 'Well, I don't know if he'll be there, Randolph. I will say it's highly likely.'

Randolph tossed his head.

'Well, yes, but he'll probably be on the roof. That's usually where Santa leaves the sleigh, isn't it?'

Randolph stamped his hoof, twice.

'You don't even have to talk to him,' said Tricksie. 'Just be the better reindeer, OK? The *bigger* reindeer. And I do mean that literally, but also metaphorically and emotionally and festively and spiritually . . .'

Randolph whined.

'Don't worry, if he tries any of his usual antics, I'll bop him right on that big red nose.'

The reindeer nodded glumly.

Tricksie turned round. 'All right, Bishops, hold on tight. We're about to go very fast, and I don't need to remind you there are no seat belts or any kind of safety precautions aboard this –'

'Absolutely not!' George's father flung himself from the reindeer with reckless abandon. He fell on his hands and knees, scrabbled to his feet and quickly backed away from them. 'I'm not going anywhere else with you,' he panted. 'Even if I have to walk home in my pyjamas!'

'Well, that was dramatic,' said Tricksie. 'We would have just let you off.'

George's father raised his finger in accusation. 'I'm not taking any more chances with you. George, Mum, come on. We're not going to Scotland. We're going home.'

'Oh, I'm very much going to Scotland,' said Nana Flo, thoroughly unruffled by her son's dismount. 'For one thing, I haven't nearly adventured enough. And, for another, I'm fantastic at hostage negotiations.'

'Right, I don't even want to get into what that means, Mum.' George's father peered up at him. 'You'll come down, won't you, George? We can go home and light a nice fire. I'll put on some soup, make some cheese toasties.'

George hesitated. He looked between his nan and his father.

'It's up to you, George,' said Tricksie, reading his thoughts. 'You can either come on an exciting adventure with the most fun crew of miscreants you'll ever meet in your life or you can go home with Mr Misery Guts over there.'

It really was a no-brainer. George desperately wanted to go on another adventure, to gallop off to Scotland with his nan and meet the little girl who had managed to capture Santa Claus himself. But, then, why did his stomach feel all hollow and strange?

'George?' said his father. Suddenly, he seemed so small, quivering below them in his dressing gown. He looked more like a lost boy than an angry businessman. 'Are you coming home with me?'

Nana Flo laid a hand on George's shoulder. 'You don't have to come with us if you don't want to, love.'

'I *do* want to go with you,' said George. 'But I don't want Dad to be alone on Christmas Day.'

'He doesn't even believe in Christmas Day,' huffed Tricksie.

'I know,' said George quietly. 'But I do. And I don't think he should be by himself.'

George's father cleared his throat, looked at his slippers. 'Yes, well, I think it would be best . . . that is to say *safer* . . . for us to be together. At home.'

In that moment, that was all George wanted. To go home with his father and get warm. He had had his fill of arguments and disappointment. He just wanted it all to be over.

Nana Flo's face softened as she looked between them. 'You two go together, then. I'll continue on as a lone wolf. I bet I'll be back before you know it.'

Perhaps it was George's imagination but Randolph's fur seemed to be getting brighter again. Reluctantly, George swung his leg over and slid off the reindeer. His father caught him as he came down. Hugo looked tired in the morning light, the circles under his eyes like two grey splodges. 'Solid ground at long last, eh?'

'Yeah,' said George, not quite able to return his smile.

Tricksie stepped up to the antlers. 'Right, then. On we go. For Christmas and country!'

'For Christmas and country!' shouted Nana Flo, kicking her legs out.

One minute they were standing on the pavement beside George and his father, and the next they were galloping down the street at breakneck speed, Randolph blurring to a giant streak of vibrant purple before their eyes. There was a flash of bright light, a delighted *yelp!* and then they disappeared entirely, leaving George and his father gaping after them.

20

The Grey Man

George's father dug his hands in his pockets. He looked at his feet while he walked, too tired now to offer even a morsel of conversation. It seemed, suddenly, there was nothing else to say. George fell into step with him, their arms brushing as they ambled home in their pyjamas.

When they reached the end of the street, a tall man appeared from round the corner and crashed straight into them. His newspaper fell with a *splat!*, the pages fanning out across the footpath. George bent down to pick them up, pausing when he noticed the date on the front page. *1843*. He looked up, past wire-framed spectacles, into a familiar pair of ice-blue eyes.

He gasped. 'You're –'

'In a frightful rush!' The man gathered up his newspaper, and bunched the pages under his arm. There was one spread still languishing on the street. 'You may keep that piece,' he said, stepping over it. 'I'm quite done with it.'

He dashed away, his heels click-clacking down the street, where he dipped round another corner and promptly disappeared.

George's father stared after him. 'Strange man.'

George picked up the discarded paper. It was an old recipe for a carrot cake with boiled icing. Someone had drawn an accompanying pencil sketch in the margin, which didn't look particularly appealing, but George's gaze was drawn to the words underneath it.

Like any good cake, the secret is in the layers. In the case of carrot cake, three is the magic number.

George's father yanked the paper from his hands. 'Don't touch that, George. It's dirty.' He scrunched it into a ball and stuffed it into a nearby bin. 'Come on. We don't want the neighbours to see us out and about in our pyjamas.'

Up ahead, George spied the familiar park railings across from his house. 'I think it's a bit late for that, Dad.'

The festivities had already spilled out on to the streets. Farah Taylor had a new puppy, and was parading him along the neighbourhood for everyone to see. Dylan and Christopher Joyce were out kicking a football around with their American cousins. Amita Kingsley was teetering on a brand-new yellow bicycle, while her father jogged along beside her, holding the back of her saddle. Mr Dubicki was going for his morning walk, singing along loudly to the music in his headphones.

George felt like he was peering into a snow globe. Here was a world full of unbridled joy – laughter that bubbles and grins that ache – that was just out of reach. He thought of Marley's cake recipe balled up in the bin – three is the magic number – and of the Christmas cracker waiting for him over at Cratchit Close. He wondered how many more years would pass before his cousins cleared that space at the end of the table, and gave up on him for good.

He decided then and there that he never wanted to find out.

He hung back, and slipped the snow globe from his pocket. While his father hurried for home, George shook it one last time. With *feeling*.

'I want my dad to see how grey a world without Christmas really is,' he whispered to the snowman. 'I want him to understand how much we've lost by getting rid of it. But, most of all, I want him to *change*.'

The snow globe warmed instantly. George pulled the sleeve of his dressing gown over his hand to keep it from burning him. Then he waited, and waited.

And *waited*.

When the flash came, he was expecting it.

His father stopped walking. 'Did you see that?' he called, his gaze trained on the sky. 'It looked like lightning.'

George stuffed the snow globe in his pocket. 'Nope.'

Somewhere in the distance, church bells were ringing. They chimed slowly and out of sync, as if they were running out of battery.

'That's . . . unusual . . .' said George's father.

A strange mist curled up from the drains and clung to the lamp posts. The faraway hum of traffic died, and, in the branches of Ebenezer Park, the birds fell out of their songs. The football rolled away, and the children stopped laughing. The air turned dense and damp, and the sky disappeared behind a canopy of fog.

George's father turned on the heel of his slipper, grimacing. 'Why does it suddenly smell like my old golf shoes?'

The church bells ended abruptly, the final broken *gong!* reverberating around them. The fog hung like a curtain now, the world hidden away behind it.

Uh oh.

George was seized by a creeping sense of doom. It suddenly felt like he had made a terrible mistake. Now, the only sound was his breath bulleting out of him and the frantic shuffle of his slippers as he hurried along the street. 'Dad?' he called out.

A hand reached out through the mist and pulled him close. 'What's happening?' his father said, his eyes wide with fear.

George took the snow globe from his pocket to find it had fogged up, too. 'I . . . I shook it. And then . . . the world stopped.'

George's father swallowed. 'Did you *ask* it to stop?'

George shook his head slowly. 'I don't think so.'

'When are you going to learn not to mess with things you don't understand, George?' George's father stuck his hand out. 'Here, let me have it.'

George curled the snow globe into his chest. 'Why?'

'Because I don't trust it,' he said, his voice anxious now. The dark smudges under his eyes were growing. 'It's dangerous.'

'It's not going to hurt us,' said George, but he wasn't feeling so certain about that now. The world around them might be magical, but this was a scary kind of magic, the sort that made his stomach churn.

'I'll keep it with me anyway,' said his father. 'Just in case.'

George handed the snow globe over. 'Yeah, OK,' he said, feeling a bit relieved.

His father dropped it into his pocket. 'Stay close to me,' he said, laying a warm hand on George's shoulder. 'We're almost home.'

The silence was eerie, the sound of their footsteps echoing too loudly. The fog had turned the world grey, and the longer they walked, the more it felt like they had stumbled into a horror movie. George was starting to notice the absence of other things. Not just people, but birds and trees and cars, too. Even the street markings had disappeared. 'Where is everyone?' he whispered. 'And everything?'

'You tell me,' said his father, looking around them. 'You wished it all away.'

'I didn't *mean* to.'

'*Listen.*' George's father grabbed his hand. 'Do you hear that?'

There was a sudden patter of footsteps. A man in a black hat and a long black coat came striding out of the fog, and walked right past them.

'Marley?' said George, scurrying after him. 'Can you help us? We're lost.'

The man ignored him.

'Hang on just a second, Marley!' shouted George's father. 'We're talking to you!'

The man only quickened his steps. He kept his head down as he walked, his hands stuck deep into his coat pockets.

'I don't think he can hear us,' said George, with dawning alarm.

'He's just ignoring us,' said his father, quickening his pace. 'He's the one who put us here.'

When they caught up with the man, he was hurrying up the steps to a house. There was a crooked 7 on the door. He stuck his key in the lock, and it swung open.

'Hey! This is our house!' George raced up the steps and stuck his foot out to keep the door from closing. They slipped inside after the man, and the door slammed shut behind them.

George blinked, his eyes adjusting to the dimness. The walls were tombstone grey. So was the ceiling and the floors, even the plant by the front door. 'What's going on?'

George saw the fear paling his father's face. 'Wait here, George. I'll handle this.' He stiffened his spine, then stalked down the hallway with his arms swinging by his sides. 'This is my house! You can't just walk in here!'

George crept down the hall and ducked his head round the door to the kitchen. The colour had been leeched from in here, too.

Uh oh.

In the living room, the portrait of Walter Bishop was still hanging above the fireplace, but it had been repainted in shades of grey. Walter wasn't smiling any more, either. In fact, he looked sterner than ever. His brow was heavy, his mouth pressed into a hard line as he looked off into the middle distance. George's hands slickened with sweat. His pulse was hammering in his ears. It looked like the entire house had been run through the washing machine one too many times.

He was about to call out for his father, when he noticed him standing over by the window. He was scrolling through his phone.

'That was quick,' said George. 'Did you find Marley?'

His father ignored him.

George froze. It was only then that he noticed his father's crisp business suit, his tight-laced shiny shoes. In a matter of minutes, he had changed out of his dressing gown. Even his hair was neat again, and slicked behind his ears. But, stranger still, everything about him – right down to the hue of his skin – was ashen. He looked like he had just walked out of a black-and-white movie.

George's cheeks began to prickle. 'D-dad?' he said, edging closer. 'C-can you hear me?'

The man lifted his phone to his ear.

'What do you mean?' came a voice from behind George. 'Of course I can hear you.'

George turned to find his father, dishevelled and pyjama'd, standing in the threshold to the living room.

George's knees shook as he shuffled aside. 'Dad, if you're here,' he whispered, 'then who is that man by the window?'

George's father's eyes widened with horror. He pressed a finger to his lips as he stepped into the room. He tiptoed over to the fireplace, and grabbed the metal poker from its stand.

The Grey Man began to yell down the phone.

'He sounds just like you, Dad,' said George, as they crept up on him. 'Even the way he moves his hands is the same.'

The Grey Man was gesticulating wildly, so caught up in his tirade that a stampede of wildebeest could have gone unnoticed behind him. 'I don't *care* if it takes you the entire day. Save your sob story for someone who has time!'

George's father nodded at George, then raised the poker like a baseball bat. 'All right, sir. Turn round and explain yourself *immediately* and no one gets hurt!' he demanded loudly.

'Well, I don't believe in Christmas!' snapped the man.

'He can't hear you,' said George, daring to edge even closer. 'We're invisible to him. Like we were in the other miracles.'

George's father lowered his poker. 'So, he's a ghost, then. One of Marley's, I suppose.' He snorted. 'Does he really expect me to be frightened of *myself*?'

'I don't know,' said George uneasily. 'Maybe he wants you to —'

The Grey Man spun round suddenly, a flailing hand nearly hitting George in the face. '. . . a pointless, money-wasting, emotionally draining holiday!' he ranted. 'I've told you a thousand times. I don't care about Christmas and neither does this company. The world still turns and you must keep up with it!'

George peered up into the Grey Man's face, and felt the colour drain from his own. 'D-dad,' he said, his voice trembling. 'D-do you s-see w-what I see?'

George's father swayed a little, as though he was about to pass out. '*No*,' he said, the word soundless on his lips. 'No, no, *no*.'

The Grey Man wasn't Hugo Bishop at all.

It was George.

21

A Gloomy Fate

George stumbled backwards, his stomach hollowing as if he had been punched. 'We're in the *future*,' he breathed. '*My future*.'

His father's mouth was bobbing open and closed like a fish. He swivelled on his heel, taking in the grey room. Gone were all traces of Hugo and Nana Flo. The bookshelves were dusty, the fireplace bricked up. There was only a single armchair in the corner, a laptop sitting on its side table. 'It's so –'

'Empty,' said George in a small voice. 'I've become a *Scrooge*.'

Gong! Gong! Gong!

The church bells were ringing again. Outside, the fog was clearing. There came the distant sound of laughter, and, just beyond it, the telltale twinkle of the Christmas tree in Ebenezer Park.

The Grey Man moved towards the window.

As if drawn by an invisible magnet, George and his father moved with him.

The streets were full again, families wandering with their children, neighbours exchanging Christmas greetings.

A snowball whizzed past the window.

George looked down to see a familiar face skipping down the street. She was older now – by many years – but he would have known that smile anywhere. It was Clementine. A snowball hurtled into her shoulder. She spun round. Bobbie ducked behind the pram she was pushing, giggling into her hand. The young man beside her splayed his arms, as if to say, *Don't look at me.*

The Grey Man made a strange choking noise – it was the chuckle of someone who didn't quite know how to laugh. It died in his throat, and when George looked up he found him stern-faced. His grey eyes looked haunted, and he was wearing a frown George didn't recognize.

Because I haven't learned it yet, he thought.

SPLAT!

A snowball exploded against the windowpane.

Clementine was standing on the steps of 7 Ebenezer Street. She looked up, a gloved hand shielding her eyes from the sun's glare. Then she waved.

The Grey Man inhaled sharply, moved away from the window.

George laid his forehead against the glass and closed his eyes, pretending he was a million light years from this awful place and its sickly, creeping loneliness.

Down below, Bobbie drifted towards her sister. '. . . all we know, he's not even there.'

'He *is*,' Clementine insisted. 'I saw him.'

'I'm not sure why we keep coming here, Clem. We're wasting our time.'

'And why do you keep dragging me along?' asked the young man. 'I don't even *know* him.'

'Because he's your cousin too, Tim,' said Clem.

'George,' came his father's voice, close to his ear. 'Come away from the window.'

'No.' George swallowed. 'I want to hear.'

But their voices faded, and when George opened his eyes again the fog had returned. It was thicker and greyer than before. He turned away from the window, to find the Grey Man had disappeared.

His father began to pace. 'Don't worry, son. I'm going to get us out of here right now,' he said, slipping the snow globe from his pocket and holding it up like a beacon. 'Marley is not going to have the last laugh.'

George stared in dismay at the snow globe. The snowman had disappeared. It was just an empty bubble now, like the house in which they stood. He sank on to the window ledge. 'I don't think anyone is laughing, Dad.'

His father shook the snow globe. 'Why isn't it working?'

He shook it harder, his face getting redder and redder. 'Last time, I shook it really hard and it got the message.'

'Last time we almost died in an avalanche,' said George, rolling to his feet. 'Don't do that.'

'I *have* to. It's not fair on us. It's not fair on you.' George's father's hand was moving so fast, it blurred. The room began to tremble. A light bulb dropped from the ceiling and shattered at their feet.

'Dad! Stop it!' George jumped for the snow globe, but his father leapt backwards.

'It's too dangerous, George. Let me do it.' The bookshelf toppled over, spitting dusty jackets across the floor. The fireplace spat its bricks out. The curtain pole fell, dragging the curtains down with it.

'Look where you're going!' warned George.

'I know where we're going. *Home.*' His father's eyes were alight, his hair sticking up in every direction. He was swinging his arm round and round, the floorboards trembling violently beneath them. 'Do you see this, Marley?' he yelled. 'This is me breaking apart your cruel little experiment. This is me saying *no* to your games. This is me protecting my son!'

'DAD!'

There was a sudden *crack* and a faint *whoosh*. George's father's eyes went wide as his feet connected with the spine of a book. His slippers shot up like flippers, his heels pedalling for purchase against the floor. The book slid out from under him and he careened backwards, the snow globe flying from his grip and soaring through the air.

George lunged, but it was too late.

His father crashed to the floor.

The snow globe hurtled into the wall and smashed into a million pieces.

22

The Shattered Snow Globe

George knelt in the shards of his last-minute miracle. There was glass everywhere. A syrupy liquid was bubbling out, slipping into the cracks between the floorboards. 'You *broke* it, Dad.'

'No, no, no, *no*,' said George's father, his knees creaking as he crawled towards George. When he beheld the mess, his face crumpled. 'I didn't mean to. I swear, George. I was just trying to bring us home. I just wanted to make it stop.'

George started picking up the pieces of Marley's snow globe, one by one by one. He salvaged even the tiniest chippings; the glass so fine he could barely see it. His father passed him his hanky, and George carefully folded the unmakings of his miracle into it, before slipping it into the pocket of his dressing gown. The globe might be broken, but George hoped the magic wasn't completely lost.

When George took his hand from his pocket, his skin was the pale grey of a winter sky, and ice cold. A quick glance at the mirror by the bookshelf showed the colour fading from his cheeks. He looked at his father. He was turning grey, too – everything from the rings under his eyes right down to the belt loops on his dressing gown.

George's father was looking back at him with the same horror. He brought his hands to his mouth. 'George. You've gone all grey.'

Perhaps it was the shattered miracle in his pocket or the terrifying realization that the grey world had risen up to claim them, but George Bishop decided in that moment that he couldn't take it any more.

A fierce anger took hold of him, hot and stirring as a volcano. He opened his mouth and it erupted.

'I told you to be careful!' he burst out. 'And you didn't listen. You *never* listen to me.'

'I was only trying to help,' his father protested weakly.

'No, *I* was trying to help,' said George, sweeping his hand around. 'That's what I've been doing all along, Dad. But it hasn't worked. Because you can't force someone to be happy if they refuse to be, and you can't stop a Scrooge from being a Scrooge no matter how hard you try!' George sucked in a breath. 'You thought the Grey Man was a ghost, well you're a ghost, too. You've been a ghost for three years. You wear my dad's face but you don't act like him. You don't smile or laugh any more. And you never talk about *Mum*.'

George's father dragged his hands across his jaw. 'What is there to say, George?' he said sadly. 'She's not here.'

'But *I'm* here, Dad.' George pressed his hand against his chest, to keep his heart from bursting. '*I'm* still here. And I want to talk about her.' His voice cracked; when he spoke again his words were watery. 'I want to remember her.'

'I've given you everything I can,' said George's father. 'A roof over your head. Food and clothes and warmth, all the things you've ever needed. What more could you possibly want?'

'I want you to *live*!' pleaded George.

His father blinked.

A rush of tears rolled down George's cheeks. 'When Mum died, I didn't think that you would die, too. But that's what it feels like. This grey world might scare you, but it doesn't scare me. I'm *used* to it. Life lost its colour a long time ago. All

I'm trying to do is get it back.' His shoulders slumped. 'But I give up, Dad.'

George's father made a strangled noise, like the words he wanted to say were all getting stuck in his throat. He looked suddenly very frightened.

George couldn't stand to look at him. To bear his own pain was one thing, but to see it reflected back at him was too much. He shot to his feet, and hurried out into the hallway.

'George!' his father called after him. 'Wait! Please!'

George was tired of waiting. Before he could think better of it, he swung the front door open and walked out into the fog.

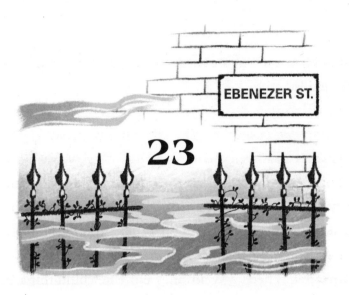

The Devouring Fog

The mist threw its arms round George.

'Marley?' he called out.

Marley, Marley, Marley, the fog echoed back.

'I know you're here somewhere!'

Somewhere, somewhere, somewhere!

George made it across the street only to find the park had disappeared. There was just a desert of tarmac now, the fog rising from the ground like steam. It curled up the legs of his pyjamas and pressed a chill into his bones. He spun round, searching for a break in the mist.

'Hello?'

Hello? Hello? Hello?

George swallowed a rush of panic. Marley was nowhere to be found. Perhaps this really was the end of their miracle, and he was stuck here forever. It certainly felt like it. He traced his footsteps back the way he had come, but when he reached the other side of Ebenezer Street, the houses had disappeared. There was nothing but the rolling clouds, the echo of his heartbeat thundering in his ears.

'Hello!' he yelled. 'Is anyone out there?'

Out there? Out there? Out there?

From somewhere far, far away, George heard his father's voice.

'George? Can you hear me?'

'George! Where are you?'

George spun round again, tracking the sound of his father's voice. He could hear the terror in it, the same sickening feeling that the world was ending and they were melting away with it. 'Dad! Where are you?'

'Follow my voice, George!'

Follow my voice!

Follow my voice!

Follow my voice!

Suddenly, George's father's voice was everywhere. It swooped down from the sky and hitchhiked on the wind. George thundered towards the first echo, only to find the next one further away than before.

'George!'

George!

George!

George!

George found himself dwarfed beneath a blank-faced house. It wound up and up and up, into the clouds. He turned round, only to find another one looming over him. The street was shrinking. The houses inched closer, boxing him in. The windows grew narrow and hunched, shadows flickering from within. 'Dad, the buildings are moving!'

'Come away from them!' shouted his father, his voice floating up from the street drains. 'I'm at the park, George! Can you see it?'

'Stay there! I'm coming!' George hurried down the narrowing street, the footpaths clipping his ankles. The toe of his slipper caught on a kerb, and he went down hard on his hands and knees. He couldn't hear his father any more. The mist had swallowed him up. Now George was alone, out of breath and out of bravery. He started to cry, his tears dripping down his cheeks and turning the grey of his skin silver. 'Please, someone help me,' he croaked.

When he stood up, the houses had all tumbled away like Jenga blocks. The landscape rolled away from him in an endless plain of grey. It was as if the whole world had been whipped out from underneath him like a tablecloth. Now, he was the only one left.

George was utterly and hopelessly alone.

24

The Sound of Home

George wiped his cheeks on his sleeve, but the tears kept coming hot and fast. After a while, he simply gave up, and wandered on, into the mist. '*Please*,' he whispered, his voice too loud in the silence. 'I just want to be with my dad.'

The fog was so dense he could barely see his hands in front of his face.

A faint heat prickled against his hip. The broken snow globe was glowing softly. Being careful of the sharp glass, he held his hand against the outside of his dressing-gown pocket.

He moved a couple of steps, and the globe grew warmer. *Hope.*

'*Please*,' said George. 'Help me find my way home.'

Another few steps and it got hotter still.

George let the shattered snow globe guide him through the fog. When the glass got colder, he came to an abrupt stop. He turned to the left. A flare of warmth. Another step. Warmer still. He walked ten paces before the snow globe lost its heat. He turned left again. Another flare.

'George?' his father was calling for him, somewhere just beyond the veil of mist. He sounded like he was about to throw up. 'Are you there, Georgie?'

The snow globe flared.

The message was clear: *keep going.*

So George did.

'George, can you hear me?'

Another flare, this one even hotter than before.

The snow globe was responding to the sound of his father's voice! Hope quickened George's steps, his breath wheezing out of him. Home wasn't a place; it was a person. The snow globe was leading him to his dad.

'I'm coming, Dad!' Twelve more paces. A prickle of ice. George turned again, tracking towards his dad's echo. The glass got hotter. Eight paces. Another flare of heat, and on it went, George zigzagging across the square, until Ebenezer Park appeared through a break in the fog.

George trailed his fingers along the railings to keep them from disappearing. When he reached the gates, they creaked open on their own. George's father was doubled over on the park bench. His arms were wrapped round his middle as though he had an awful stomach ache, and he was tapping his right foot very quickly against the ground.

'Dad?'

George's father snapped his head up. His eyes were puffy, and his hair was a mess. He leapt to his feet, and pulled George into a hug. 'Oh, thank goodness!' He was trembling from head to toe, his heartbeat hammering against George's cheek. 'I thought I'd lost you!'

'Me too,' sobbed George. 'I thought I'd be on my own forever.'

'I'd never let that happen, Georgie,' said his father, his warm breath ruffling George's hair. '*Never.*'

'I shouldn't have gone looking for Marley.'

'I shouldn't have let you go,' said his father, pulling back from him. He braced his hands on George's shoulders as though to keep him from disappearing again. 'I should have *listened* to you.' He closed his eyes, trying to scrunch the tears away. 'I'm so sorry, Georgie. I'm sorry it took a miracle. *Three* miracles! And I'm sorry I broke the snow globe.' He flinched. 'I want you to live in colour. I want to live in colour with you. It's what your mum would have wanted.'

George and his father huddled together in their pyjamas, and, after a little while, George noticed that the fog was beginning to melt away.

George and his father made their way home. Though the creeping mist had finally cleared, there appeared to be no life hiding underneath it. There were no children playing outside, no faces at the windows, no church bells peeling in the distance. There wasn't a hint of blue in the sky. The houses had returned to their rightful places but they didn't quite look the same. When George and his father returned to 7 Ebenezer Street, the front door was swinging on its hinges. In the living room, Walter Bishop was still frowning in his portrait, as colourless as the world around him.

'We're stuck.' George's father sank into the armchair and pressed his face into his hands. 'Stuck in this *awful* place.'

'But the miracle *worked*,' said George, more to the walls than to his father. 'You saw. You learned. You *cried*.'

His father looked at him through his fingers. 'I was too late,' he said in a muffled voice. 'I'm sorry, George.'

George perched on the armrest and took his father's hand. 'We're not giving up,' he said, squeezing tight. 'We've come way too far. And it's still Christmas, somewhere. That means there's still hope. There's still *magic*.'

George's father shook his head, defeated.

It was up to George now. He leapt to his feet. 'Marley!' he yelled, as he paced across the room. 'Come out, Marley! I know you're here!'

A bell tinkled through the doorway, the trill as faint as a bee's sneeze. George hurried out of the living room to find Coco sitting in the middle of the hallway, staring at him. 'Where did you come from?'

Coco was wearing a tiny Christmas jumper. It was bright red, with two golden bells in the middle. Round her neck she wore a miniature version of them.

'And where did you get that jumper?' said George suspiciously.

Coco turned round and trotted down the hallway. The bells tinkled over her shoulder, bidding George to follow. When Coco reached his bedroom, she pawed at the door. It opened with a *creak!* and a pine-scented gust slipped out.

George walked inside after her.

25

The Curious Bedroom Shop

'Close the door, will you?' came a familiar voice. 'You'll let all the colour out.'

George shut the door and pressed his back against it. His bedroom had been completely transformed. The ceiling was strung with multicoloured fairy lights and reams of tinsel. The floor was carpeted with fresh pine needles, the air dusted with the scent of evergreen. There were garlands draped along shelves that shouldn't be there, glass birds chirping from faraway perches. Beside George, a plinth of tuxedo-wearing gingerbread men stood up all on their own, as if to usher him inside.

'Age?' Across the shop, in the spot where George's bed used to be, Marley was sitting at his desk. His newspaper was open in front of him, his glasses perched on the tip of his nose. He was nibbling on a candy cane.

'It's me. George Bishop,' said George uncertainly. 'You're in my house?'

'*Age?*' Marley repeated.

'Ten and four months?' said George. 'We've met before.'

Marley narrowed his eyes. 'I don't recognize you. Did you have a moustache?'

George, sensing a game was afoot, narrowed his eyes right back. 'Where's my bed gone?'

'We don't sell beds,' said Marley. 'But perhaps you'll find something else that tickles your fancy.'

'No. I mean, what's your shop doing in my bedroom?' George clarified.

Marley wagged the candy cane at him. 'I think the better question, George, is, what's your bedroom doing in my shop?'

George opened his mouth, then closed it again. He turned on the heel of his slipper, spotting the familiar shelves WHAT IF? and WHY NOT?, which bookended a collection of inanimate wooden elves. They all looked very much like Tricksie, but

George knew, without knowing quite how, that they weren't *his* Tricksie.

When he looked up, past a bay stuffed with novelty Christmas hats, he spotted the sleeve of his school jumper peeking out from the top of his wardrobe. His bedroom window was exactly where it always was, though Marley had covered it with a giant photograph of himself, entitled *Employee of the Century*.

Coco trotted past in her Christmas jumper, the bells on her collar tinkling. 'If this isn't my bedroom, then what's my cat doing here?'

Marley regarded Coco over the bridge of his spectacles. 'That's my cat.'

'You don't have a cat,' George reminded him.

Marley nibbled on his candy cane. 'Well, why is she wearing one of my Christmas jumpers then?'

'I don't know. Did you put her in it?'

'It's possible,' Marley admitted. 'There's nothing sadder to me than an unfestive animal.'

BANG BANG BANG!

'George!' George's bedroom door swung open, and Hugo Bishop filled up the frame like a spectre. 'What on earth is going on?'

'Age?' said Marley.

George's father tried to enter the room but he couldn't quite seem to step over the threshold. His palms flattened against an invisible wall. 'What is this?' he demanded. 'Let me in!'

Marley adjusted the spectacles on his nose to take a closer look at him. '*Age?*' he said again.

'Dad,' hissed George. 'That's Marley. You have to tell him your age.'

George's father levelled Marley with a dark look. 'Oh, it's *you*,' he said accusingly. 'Do you have *any* idea how many times you've nearly killed us with your high jinks?'

'I won't ask you again,' said Marley, wagging his candy cane.

'Forty-two!' snapped George's father, still pushing against the invisible wall. 'Now, let me in!'

'Forty-two?' said Marley, aghast. 'Good grief. Absolutely *not*.'

Before George's father could answer, Marley flicked his wrist and the door slammed shut in his face. 'Right, then,' he said, setting his candy cane down and offering George his full, undivided attention. 'What brings you to my shop today?'

George was conscious of his father yelling on the other side of the door, his fists pounding uselessly against the wood. Somehow, Hugo's cries were getting fainter and fainter, as though Marley was turning his volume down.

'My dad and I are stuck in a broken miracle,' said George.

'Oh *dear*,' said Marley, pressing a hand to his cheek.

George wasn't fully convinced by his surprise. 'The snow globe isn't working any more,' he explained anyway. 'I need something that will get us back home. To our real house. In our real world.'

'You certainly do,' agreed Marley, and George was relieved, at least, to be taken seriously. 'And the sooner the better, I might add. Miracle-lag is no joke. The time difference can give you awful whiplash. Do you have the snow globe with you?'

George stuck his hand into his pocket and carefully removed the hanky. He laid the broken shards of his last-minute miracle, very gently, across Marley's desk.

Marley stared at the shards for a very long time, his frown growing deeper and deeper. 'Oh no,' he muttered, shaking his head. 'No, no, no, no. This won't do at all.'

'What is it?' said George anxiously.

Marley reached under his desk and grabbed a miniature wooden sign. He set it down on the desk with a *thud*, sending the glass shards flying.

It read:

NO REFUNDS ON BROKEN CURIOSITIES. EVER.

George swallowed. 'But it was an accident.'

Marley spun the sign round.

On the back it read:

ACCIDENTS ARE NOT EXCUSES.

George stared at the shards of his miracle, his heart plummeting in his chest. 'But what am I supposed to do now?'

Marley shrugged. 'I'm a shopkeeper, not a therapist. Buy something else.'

George looked down at his crumpled pyjamas, his stained dressing gown. 'But I don't have any money. Can I – Can I see if my dad can lend me some?'

Without a word, Marley shook his head.

George backed away from the desk. 'Well, what now?' He looked around the shop, where Christmas dripped from the ceiling like icicles. Bejewelled headpieces winked at him from far-off shelves. In the corner of the room, a tower of fudge teetered like the Leaning Tower of Pisa. Beside it, a row of rocking horses watched George with sapphire eyes.

'I can't just live *here* forever,' cried George.

'Well, of course you can't,' said Marley, chuckling at the preposterousness of such an idea. 'For one thing, we close at 6.43 p.m. sharp every day. And, for another, the last child who stowed away in here ate me out of twelve years' worth of chocolate coins.' He shook his head at the memory. 'I had to put Tricksie on probation for taking in another stray.'

'So Dad and I have to live in the grey world forever?'

Marley opened his newspaper. 'I'm afraid that's the nature of consequences, George,' he said, ruffling the pages. 'I don't make the rules; I just put them on placards.'

George tried to scrunch his tears back but they slipped out anyway, and trailed down his cheeks. In trying to save his father with the snow globe, he had doomed them both. The second he walked out of Marley's shop, they would be stuck forever.

In a place without colour.

A world without any traces of his mum.

Coco trotted out from under a shelf, mewing pathetically.

George sank to his knees. 'I'm sorry, Coco,' he sniffed, as he scratched behind her ears. 'I was only trying to make things better.'

Rrrap! Rrrap! Rrrap!

George and Coco snapped their heads up just in time to watch the door creak open. A new figure appeared in the door frame, this one shorter and portlier than the last. George's dad was standing behind her on his tiptoes, trying to peer in.

George rolled to his feet. 'Nan? Is that you?'

Nana Flo stood on the threshold to Marley's shop in her dressing gown and curlers. The colour had been washed out of her too, but somehow it didn't diminish her. She fixed her hands on her hips and raised her chin expectantly.

'Age?' called Marley in a bored voice. He was behind his newspaper again, scouring the events of 1843.

Nana Flo winked at George. 'Young at heart.'

Marley laid his newspaper down. A smile curled on his lips. 'Hello, Florence.'

Nana Flo grinned. 'Hello, Marley.'

She stepped into the shop without a beat of hesitation, and the invisible wall melted away to let her through. The door closed softly behind her, shutting George's dad out again.

George's jaw dropped.

'It's been a long time,' said Marley, his blue eyes twinkling.

Nana Flo laughed. 'Much longer than I'd care to admit.'

George looked between the two of them, trying to make sense of it all. 'Hang on,' he said, marching across the shop. 'You two *know* each other?'

'We're old friends,' they said, at exactly the same time.

George startled. 'Well, that's . . . surprising.'

Nana Flo arched a slender brow. 'Is it?'

In fact, the more George thought about it, the more he wondered whether it was really a surprise at all. For as long as he had known her, Nana Flo had worn mystery like a cloak, her green eyes always shining with some delectable secret. She was about as close to magic as a human being could be. 'Actually, no.' He relented. 'Come to think of it, it makes perfect sense.'

'Marley and I met in Dublin many, many years ago,' Nana Flo explained. 'I believe it was in Temple Bar, wasn't it?'

'My shop was just a stall then,' said Marley wistfully. 'I was a young inventor with big dreams, a tacky suit and a jarful of magic.'

'I quite liked your suit,' said Nana Flo thoughtfully. 'Not many people can pull off fluorescent green.'

'Well, indeed,' said Marley, and, though it was dim inside the curiosity shop that had once been his bedroom, George could have sworn the old man was blushing.

'Right,' said Nana Flo, gesturing to the broken glass on Marley's desk. 'Let's get down to business, then.'

'Broken miracle.' Marley tutted under his breath. 'Terrible business. And by all accounts it was going quite well.'

'So Hugo told me,' said Nana Flo. 'I suppose there's still no exchanges on broken items?'

Marley shook his head. 'I don't make the rules . . .'

'You just put them on placards,' finished Nana Flo. 'I suppose it can't be helped.'

'We're stuck here, Nan,' said George flatly.

Nana Flo wrapped her arm round George's shoulder and pulled him close. 'We just need to find a way to get home, love.'

George patted his pockets. 'We can't. None of us brought any money with us.'

'Well, you brought me,' said Nana Flo brightly. 'And I've got something much better than money.'

She reached up and slid her holly hairclip out from between two curlers. It was then that George noticed the *pop* of colour. It shone all the brighter in her pale hand, the red berries glowing like precious jewels.

Nana Flo slid the hairclip across the counter. 'How about an exchange, Marley? I know it's been a long time, but as you can see it's still in mint condition.'

Marley plucked the hairclip from the counter, his eyes growing wide behind his spectacles. '*A Fortune Fastener*,' he breathed. 'Why, these are as rare as a purple reindeer. Are you quite sure you want to trade this, Florence?'

'Absolutely positive.' Nana Flo smiled at George. 'I've had all the fortune in the world.'

Marley handled the *Fortune Fastener* like it was a fragile baby bird. He cupped it in his hands, wrapped it in a silver cloth, then another cloth, then a drawstring pouch. He put the pouch in a big wooden box then set the wooden box in a giant safe underneath the counter. When he was done stowing it away, he returned his attention to George.

'Seeing as your returned item is top-end, vintage and in pristine condition –' he paused to dip his chin gratefully at Nana Flo – 'you may choose any single item in the shop to replace it.'

'*Really?*' said George.

Marley nodded. 'Choose wisely.'

'Go on, Georgie,' said Nana Flo encouragingly. 'If anyone can get us out of this strange old place, it's you.'

'Right.' George tightened his dressing gown and balled his fists. 'I'll do my best.'

26

The Most Important Decision in the World

George began at LAST-MINUTE MIRACLES, studying each snow globe carefully. There were whole cities enshrined in glass bubbles. There was Notre Dame sitting like a glittering throne, a boy in a red raincoat waiting patiently on its steps. In another, the Sydney Opera House was surrounded by crystal blue water and tiny speedboats. One was going so fast, it looked like it was flying.

'That's a sun globe,' Marley piped up. 'Christmas is a lot warmer in the southern hemisphere.'

'Oh. Cool.' George slid the sun globe back on the shelf.

In the next one, the Colosseum squatted in a wintry Rome, white and sturdy as a Christmas cake. Beside it, the Empire State Building crowned a snow globe chock-full of New York City, where everything was sprinkled silver and white. A girl and her grandfather danced across the top floor. George trailed his finger along the shelf, past cobbled streets and sleepy villages, wandering figurines all unknowingly part of their own unique miracles. One snow globe contained a child's bedroom. The walls were covered in pictures of ponies, and a little girl with dark hair was tucked up in bed. In the globe next to it, Big Ben was chiming. George could hear it faintly through the glass.

He stood back from the shelf. There was nothing here that reminded him of his family. These were other people's miracles. They weren't meant for him.

He moved on, to a shelf of *Secure Stockings*™. Each one was labelled with a big orange sticker that read: *RECALLED DUE TO THE EVOLVING SNEAKINESS OF CHILDREN.*

At WHAT IF? George recognized the tin of *Melancholic Mints* (they had had enough weeping for one year), and came to rest on a jar of *Jolly-Making Jam*. He looked to his Nana Flo.

She was leaning against the counter, smiling encouragingly at him. He was suddenly sure that if laughter was the way out, then his nan would have been more than enough to charter them home.

George tipped his head back, to where a collection of silver pipes hung from the ceiling like windchimes. '*Forgiveness Flutes*,' he read aloud. '*Play your grudges away.*'

'A new-season item,' Marley called from across the shop. 'You play one of those in your enemy's face and I defy them not to invite you in for tea.'

George considered this briefly. The truth was, his father didn't need his forgiveness. It had already been given freely. He wandered away, past a row of old-fashioned telephones with circular dials and spiralling cords. *Togetherness Telephones*, read the sign. *A lonely loved one is just a phone call away.*

'Are you having trouble choosing, love?' asked his Nan.

George spun on his heel, dwarfed by a lifetime's worth of glittering curiosities. 'There are so many options, but none of them feel right.'

'Well, I'd invite you to please hurry along,' said Marley, tapping his candy cane on the counter. 'It's almost 6.43 p.m., you know.'

George frowned. 'It was morning just a minute ago.'

'The shop keeps to its own rhythm,' said Marley, indicating the cuckoo clock on the wall. It had just turned half past six.

'Oh dear,' said Nana Flo. 'That's not much time at all, is it?'

'That's because he just sped it up,' said George accusingly.

Marley smiled blandly. 'I don't know why you're having such trouble, George. After all, it's only the most important decision in the world.'

George hurried along, scanning everything at double time. When he reached a familiar shelf of glass birds, he stopped. There were robins and larks and nightingales, all poised to sing. He trailed his finger over each one, searching for a prickle of warmth. Maybe it was his imagination but the cuckoo clock was ticking louder now. He was conscious of those seconds slipping through his fingers, all too aware of his father waiting out in the hallway, caught halfway between panic and despair.

George picked up the glass nightingale. It felt wrong in his palm. He quickly returned it to the shelf and glanced at the clock. There was less than five minutes left. He hurried back to his bedroom door and pressed his ear against it. 'Dad? Are you still there?'

There was a faint shuffling on the other side. The handle rattled but didn't turn. 'I'm here, Georgie. Are you all right in there?'

'I'm fine. Nana's here. Dad, I can pick anything I want from the shop to get us out of here, but I don't know what to choose,' said George quickly. His heartbeat thundered in his ears; his throat was bone-dry with nerves. 'Time is running out, and I'm afraid I'll make a mistake and we'll be stuck forever.'

His father pressed his forehead against the door. 'Listen to me very carefully, Georgie,' he said, his voice echoing through the wood. 'You're the wisest person I know. You always have been. You can see light in the darkness, a pathway through the densest fog and colour in a grey old grouch like me. If there's a way home, you will find it. Your heart is a compass, George. All you have to do is follow it.'

George pressed his hand against the wood, a spark of confidence taking hold inside him. 'Thanks, Dad.'

'Just do your best,' he said, his voice getting further away. 'That's all you can do.'

George sprang up and planted his feet in the middle of the shop. He closed his eyes, and though the clock was ticking all around him now, he allowed himself a deep, steadying breath. He pushed aside his anxiety, banished the prickles of fear and despair, and listened instead to his heart. The place where his mother lived.

Help me, Mum.

Bring us home.

When George opened his eyes, he was facing the largest bay in the shop. It was full of Christmas hats – tall stripy ones hung beside tiny top hats. There were bright red Santa-style creations complete with cloudy beards, and elfin ones that wound up towards the ceiling. George was about to move on, when something stopped him.

There was a slight shimmer in the air, a quiet shifting in his chest. He moved a little closer, looked a little harder.

In the middle of the bay, sitting all by itself, was a dark green hat. It wasn't shiny or brand new like the others. In fact, it was a bit crumpled and a tad sorry-looking. The rim was scuffed, the material fraying along the top. And yet George knew, right down in the deepest part of himself, that it was the most valuable item in the entire shop. Worth a hundred *Fortune Fasteners*, and three times as many snow globes.

He lunged for it, like it might fly away from him. The other hats parted to let him through, and he stumbled backwards, clutching it to his chest.

When he spun round, Nana Flo and Marley were staring at him.

'A hat,' said Marley curiously.

'Not just any hat,' said George. 'This is Dad's hat.' He swallowed the rush of emotions that came with it. 'From *before*.'

That single word held in it a world of meaning.

'Goodness,' said Nana Flo, coming to take a closer look. 'What's it doing here, then?'

'Must have found its way out of the *Lost & Found* cupboard,' said Marley suspiciously. 'Certain elves do have a habit of switching things round when I'm not looking.'

George plonked the hat on the counter. 'This, please.'

Marley frowned at it. 'What do you want me to do, wrap it in a bow? I deal in curiosities not frivolities.' He waved him away. 'Go on then, take it. Off you go.'

'That's it?' said George.

Marley shrugged, but George caught the twinkle in his eye. 'That's it.' He gestured to Coco, who was nibbling at the leaning tower of fudge. 'You may take the cat, too.'

Nana Flo plucked Coco off the floor and folded her into her arms, just as the cuckoo clock on the wall spat out an eerily realistic robin. It broke into a perfectly tuned Christmas carol.

'6.43 p.m.,' said Marley, picking up his newspaper. 'Closing time.'

All at once, the shop began to disappear. The fairy lights flickered, then vanished. The snow globes winked out. The musical instruments shimmered into thin air. The hats fell from their perches, but were gone before they hit the ground. George's dresser sprang up where the fudge tower had just been; the window creaked as Marley's poster blew away. The pine needles were swept aside to reveal the carpet beneath, the scent of evergreen carried off on a rogue breeze. The elves picked up their legs as the shelves rolled back into the walls.

And, all the while, the robin sang. Marley read his newspaper, humming along in perfect harmony.

As the counter folded down into nothing, so, too, did Marley himself. The newspaper hung a moment in mid-air and then a fierce gust came and carried it straight out of the open window. The curtains drew themselves back together, and, as George and his nan stood watching it all in muted wonder, his bed sprang up between them.

It had been lovingly made, the sheets tucked in at the sides, the pillows expertly fluffed. The robin was the last curiosity to disappear, and when it did it took the final notes of its Christmas carol with it.

'Well,' said Nana Flo, setting Coco down again. 'Say what you will about Marley, but he certainly knows how to make an exit.'

'Where do you think he's gone?' asked George, peering out the window.

'Wherever he's needed, I suppose.' Nana Flo plucked a half-eaten candy cane off the floor. 'The wheels of magic are ever-turning, after all.'

'Right then.' Still clutching the hat to his chest, George made a beeline for his bedroom door. 'Let's get ourselves out of this grey world and into one with some turkey.'

Nana Flo marched after him, grinning from ear to ear. 'My thoughts exactly.'

27

The Return of Christmas

George's father was sitting in the middle of the grey hallway, waiting for them. 'George!' he said, scrabbling quickly to his feet. 'You got out!' He threw his arms round his son and rocked him back and forth, the hug so strong it lifted George off his feet. 'Listen, I've been thinking about this grey world,' he said, setting him down again. 'If we're stuck here, then so be it. We've got each other, haven't we? I'm sure we can find a way to make it bearable. Maybe we could even make it fun! What if we sang every morning? You could draw some of your pictures, too, and hang them on the walls. And, in the evenings, we could tell stories about Mum, about the old days. We can throw our own holidays, too. We'll start with Christmas. We might not have the colour for it but what if we had the cheer, Georgie? The merriment? The *love*. I'm sure we can do that. After all, that's what really matters in the –'

He fell out of his sentence when he noticed the hat clutched to George's chest.

'Oh. That's . . .'

George held up the hat.

It was perfectly, brilliantly green.

'Mine,' said his father quietly.

George handed it to him. 'I'm not sure why I took it,' George admitted, the edges of his confidence beginning to fray. Suddenly, it seemed rather foolish to have taken nothing but a worn hat out of a glittering trove of magic, but here they were. Three exhausted adventurers, huddled in a grey hallway round the last speck of colour in the world. 'I think it's what Mum would have done.'

His father took the hat, his eyes misting as he traced the scuffed rim. 'It was your mum's first Christmas present to me.'

'Yeah,' said George, remembering her words. 'Sometimes, a spark of colour makes all the difference in the world.'

His father smiled as he placed it on his head. George marvelled as the colour returned to his face – first, the blue of his eyes, then the faint blush in his cheeks. It bled down his neck and painted the collar of his pyjama shirt, his robe and his slippers, too. Beside him, Nana Flo's robe turned pink as rose petals, the green of her eyes shining brightly behind her spectacles.

George's father began to laugh. 'What a wonderful sight!' he said, watching the colour climb the walls like ivy, hopping from one room into the next. 'You did it, George! You brought us home!'

They hurried into the living room to find it fully restored, the portrait of Walter Bishop smiling down at them once more.

'The children are back!' Nana Flo was at the window, pressing her nose against the glass. 'And just look! Farah's got a brand-new puppy!'

'Our decorations are still in the attic, you know,' said George's father, springing into action. 'Is it too late to put up the tree?'

'It's never too late,' said George, hurrying after him.

'It's never too early for a Christmas sherry either,' Nana Flo called after them. 'I'll break out my secret stash!'

They set to work, lavishing the house with colour and Christmas. Soon, the tree from the attic stood sentry by the window, glittering red and gold. The garlands were returned to the mantlepiece, tinsel wrapped round the bookcase like a scarf.

When George returned from hanging their wreath on the front door, his father was excavating another box. This one was full of photographs of their family, George's mum smiling out of each one like a sun. Her paintings were there, too, all of them more beautiful than George could remember. When they had finished decorating for Christmas, they decorated for Greta, casting her memory across the house like a spell.

When all was said and done, George and his family sank on to the couch, utterly exhausted. After three long years, Christmas had returned to 7 Ebenezer Street. The house was a home again.

Somewhere in the distance, church bells were chiming in perfect harmony.

Epilogue

When Aunt Alice opened the door to 63 Cratchit Close, she almost fainted with shock. George was surprised, too, but in a more practical sense. The door frame had been miraculously repaired, the primroses magically resprouted.

'*George*,' she gasped, as though he was a ghost come to haunt her.

She flung her arms round him and hugged him with the fierceness of three long years. When she pulled back, her eyes were wet.

'Oh, Hugo,' she said, turning to George's father. 'I knew you'd come back to us.'

George's father had gone beet red. He cleared his throat awkwardly. 'Yes, well, I hope you and Eli don't mind –'

The rest of his sentence was muffled by Aunt Alice's hug. She squeezed him so tight, he let out a strange hiccoughing noise. And then another, his face pressed so tight into her shoulder, George could only see the crown of his head. Aunt Alice's shoulders were shaking.

By the time Alice had finished embracing Nana Flo, the others were upon them. Clementine and Bobbie barrelled down the hallway, yelping with delight. They crashed into George with such force the three of them nearly fell off the doorstep. They dragged him inside by his coat sleeves, chattering at full volume. George could hardly make out a single sentence, just words like 'purple reindeer' and 'teeny tiny' and 'Christmas explosion'.

'It's been quite a mess here this morning,' said Aunt Alice as she followed them down the hall. 'The tree took a bit of a toppling earlier. We're still trying to clean up all the baubles.'

'OH REALLY?' said George's father, his voice an octave higher than normal. 'WHAT A SHAME.'

'Not to worry, Alice, love. Christmas is such a chaotic time, isn't it?' said Nana Flo smoothly. 'And especially with a new baby. It's just wonderful that we can all be together again.'

'ON THIS ENTIRELY NORMAL DAY,' said George's father, laughing awkwardly.

George nudged him in the ribs. 'Dad, you're being weird.'

'Don't worry, Uncle Hugo. They'd never believe you anyway,' added Clementine with a wink.

'Believe what?' said Uncle Eli, who was standing in the kitchen, rocking Tim back and forth. He had changed out of his nurse's uniform and was wearing a woolly jumper with a snowman on the front. 'Would you like to meet your new cousin, George?'

'Yes, please!' George folded Tim carefully into his arms.

This time, his father stood behind him, a steadying hand braced on his shoulder. 'He's beautiful,' Hugo said in a half-melted voice. 'He's got your mum's eyes.'

'Hello, Tim,' said George.

Tim blinked his big brown eyes at George, then smiled, just a little.

'Oooh, he likes you, Georgie,' said Aunt Alice. 'He was so fussy earlier.'

'HA HA, REALLY?' said George's father. 'WELL THAT'S BABIES, I SUPPOSE.'

'Sorry about him,' said Nana Flo. 'He gets a bit weird when he's hungry.'

'Well, then we should eat!' said Aunt Alice, ushering them all to sit down. 'You're just in time!'

Christmas dinner at Cratchit Close was the tastiest George could remember. The meal passed in a parade of mouth-watering dishes, and ended with a giant Christmas cake that Bobbie produced seemingly out of nowhere, much to the delight of her parents. It tasted delicious, and George enjoyed it all the better knowing it had come from Marley's curiosity shop. When dinner was finished and the tea passed out in homely mugs, they migrated to the conservatory, where Doodle sat at George's feet, nibbling companionably at his shoe.

'Who knows, maybe next year we can bring Coco along,' said Nana Flo. 'They might learn to get along?'

George's father laughed, and the sound was like music to George's ears. 'I think that'll take another miracle, Mum.'

Outside in the falling evening, an old man carrying a newspaper wandered down the street. He paused a moment outside no. 63, and listened for the echo of laughter on the wind. He smiled to himself, removed a *Forever Flake* from his pocket and hung it in the air. As the first stirrings of snow fell across the rainbow houses of Cratchit Close, the old man slipped round a corner and folded himself into the shadows. There was a patter of hooves, a tinny giggle and then a flash of purple as three Christmas-miracle makers vanished into the night.

About the Author

Catherine Doyle grew up in the West of Ireland. She has a BA in Psychology and an MA in Publishing. She is the author of the young-adult trilogy *Blood for Blood* (*Vendetta*, *Inferno* and *Mafiosa*). Her award-winning and bestselling middle-grade debut, *The Storm Keeper's Island*, is set on the magical island of Arranmore, where her grandparents grew up. The sequel, *The Lost Tide Warriors*, was published in July 2019. Catherine lives in Galway by the sea, but spends a lot of her time in London and the US.

Follow Catherine on Twitter
@doyle_cat

Q&A with author Catherine Doyle

How did you find the process of retelling this classic Christmas tale?

I was SO excited to undertake this retelling. I absolutely love Christmas. I'm one of those people who puts my tree up in November and will hold on to it well into the late days of January, until it's disintegrating all over my floor. It's my favourite time of year.

Unsurprisingly then, I'm also a huge fan of *A Christmas Carol*. Not just the original version by Charles Dickens but many of the adaptations too, including – but not limited to – *Scrooged* with Bill Murray, Jim Carrey's animated version and, my personal favourite, *A Muppet's Christmas Carol*. That one so affecting that for years I was convinced there were two Marleys in the original text.

When I sat down to write my own adaptation, I was conscious of the fact that I was not just stepping into one very big pair of shoes, but *several* big pairs of shoes. I wanted to do the story justice, but also make it my own.

I began by looking at all the elements that make the Dickens classic so special: the keen sense of place, humour, empathy, and the kind of magic that can slip through your door, appear at the window, repurpose your brass door knocker, or take you by the hand and pull you into an impossible journey. And then I thought about Marley, and how his rather startling appearance sets those three important journeys into motion – the one to Christmas past, Christmas present and Christmas future. Marley's presence became the seed of my version and it's where we begin our tale, in a mysterious little shop at the very end of a row of Christmas cabins in the heart of London's Winter Wonderland.

What challenges were there in updating a story from the Victorian era?

One of the best things about *A Christmas Carol* is how timeless the main ingredients are – the aforementioned sense of warmth, humour and empathy have very little to do with Victorian London and everything to do with the human spirit. I knew I wanted to keep all of these key ingredients but I wanted to place my story here and now, in a modern version of London that is utterly steeped in Christmas magic. I chose to tell the story through the eyes of an ordinary ten-year-old boy called George, whose world has recently been turned upside down. Now that Christmas is upon him again, all George desperately wants to do is turn the world back round. Thankfully, he has a mischievous Irish granny (is there any other kind?) who wants to help him do exactly that.

If you could design your own magical snow globe, what would it look like and what miracle would it grant?

There are a million ways to answer this question, but at this very moment I think I would like my magical snow globe to contain a miniature version of the moon. Instead of snowflakes there would be tiny silver stars that twinkle as they float, to make it look like the universe is spinning round inside. I would shake the snow globe whenever I was feeling sad or stressed or overwhelmed and in a silver flash, it would whisk me all the way up to the moon!

A
CHRISTMAS
CAROL

by

CHARLES DICKENS

'Come in, – come in!
And know me better, man!
I am the Ghost of Christmas Present.
Look upon me!
You have never seen the
like of me before!'